# MINT

by Cher Graiden

"Your question may seem silly but the fact that you asked anyway could be life changing. Always ask."

Cher 2019

# Chapter 1

Getting out of bed to get ready for work that morning was particularly challenging. My determination to become more optimistic in life, had been impeded by my distinct lack of sleep. I was wide-awake well into the early hours, reading quotes from positivity re-enforcement books, so that I could focus on achieving a more optimistic outlook in preparation for the working week. On reflection however, putting the book down earlier and going straight to sleep might have been a more sensible plan. The sad truth was these days I found it extremely difficult to sleep, I longed for the nights when I could just put my head on the pillow and fall asleep in minutes, without any effort at all. All the soothing rain noises and relaxing yoga moves, which I had attempted, albeit badly and definitely not at all like the girl in the video, had not helped at all. Even the promised 'goodnights sleep' from the herbal remedy, failed me. "You have too much going on inside your head, but nothing a hot bath and warm cup of milk wouldn't cure!" Wise words from my mother however just as ineffective, like everything else I had tried.

She was right about having too much on my mind, my life was pretty much a fiasco these days, that is post Nigel days. Nigel had been my boyfriend for three amazing years. He was always going to be 'the one' for me; I certainly saw us growing old together.

I thought life appeared to be going well for both of us, however I was certainly blinded by love and totally unprepared for what was to come. We had moved into a luxury flat together overlooking the marina in a beautiful coastal town, courtesy of his job, which made the luxury apartment easily affordable. We spent our time together strolling alongside the river during the day and in the evening, watching movies, talking about the future, drinking wine and enjoying impassioned sex. I would proudly attend posh parties as his 'significant other.' His photograph was displayed across my laptop as my screen saver, and I was always ready to introduce him as my boyfriend whenever anyone passed comment.

We had a couple's membership at an exclusive gym in the town, members on an 'invite only' basis, a double bonus in my seemingly perfect life. I wore the latest designer clothes and a weekly appointment for my hair and nails at Hot Stones, the most prestigious salon in town. Life with Nigel was amazing however on reflection, probably almost too good to be true.

I distinctly remember the day I had anticipated was going to be the best day of my life but in actually fact turned out to be an unforgettable disaster. I remember sitting in Hot Stones having my hair done, boasting to the stylist about my amazing boyfriend. I was explaining how he had been relatively quiet lately and certainly quite secretive and how I thought that perhaps he was planning some kind of surprise. "Oh my god, I bet he's going to propose!" the stylist squealed with delight. I had genuinely not let my imagination travel that far but now she had come to mention it, I too, could hardly contain my excitement. My mind started racing with the expectation as I talked her through his specific instructions for the meal that evening. My head was spinning, I felt like I was going to burst with the very idea he was on the verge of proposing marriage. He had booked a table for two in our favourite Chinese restaurant, saying he had something important to tell me, how on earth had I not anticipated this before now?

The excitement that had driven me into a state of giddy euphoria reached its dizzy heights while sitting in the taxi enroute to the restaurant. I pictured myself sauntering into the venue a paltry girlfriend and then swaggering out a fiancée. I envisioned showing off my sparkling engagement ring to family and friends and boasting of our wedding plans. As I was gazing out of the car window, it seemed as though every shop displayed photographs of weddings or wedding attire, it was like the whole universe was endorsing my pleasure and enthusiasm. When I arrived, and got out of the taxi, I gave the taxi driver an extremely generous tip, thanking him for being part of my exciting day. As I handed him the fare, he looked at me as though I was utterly insane, but I didn't care. He was entirely oblivious as to how my life was about to evolve and as it turned out, I had no more of an idea than the clueless taxi driver. Aspirations and dreams of the stunning, diamond ring and the huge wedding, were about as stable as the lazy Susan which carried the food around our table in the restaurant. As I rushed in, I caught a glimpse of Nigel sitting at a table in a cozy corner of the charming banqueting room. Everything was all so picture perfect, as I felt myself glide across the room to meet him. I sat down beaming like a Cheshire cat, on discovering he had graciously ordered our meals and already poured me a glass of red wine.

We both sat nervously waiting for what was to come; I could hardly contain my excitement as he started to speak, when the waiter arrived with the food.

It looked exquisite, despite the fact I was too excited to eat; I sipped some wine and ate a few mouthfuls. I sat anxiously awaiting his impending proposal, then came the most devastating news, crushing my hopes and dreams into a thousand million pieces. I went into a total state of shock as Nigel revealed that plans to marry me could not have been further from his mind. He said, all very matter of fact, he had arranged the meal to break the news that he had actually never loved me. In fact, he was in love with Sarah, my best friend and apparently had been for years. The fact she had discovered she was pregnant had forced them both to own up to their affair and do the decent thing for the sake of the baby, particularly in view of the impending birth.

I felt my mind and my life spinning out of control along with the egg-fried rice he had so calmly ordered earlier, as it rotated around on the lazy Susan. In just a few words, I had lost my partner, my best friend, my home and my dreams. I immediately concealed my newly manicured nails prepared specifically to receive my engagement ring. I hurriedly left the table counteracting what was said, by flippantly mumbling something about I had decided long ago our relationship was already over and in fact I was actually relieved, because I had been trying to sum up the courage to tell him I had been harboring plans to move on. This was my pathetic attempt in clawing back a slither of my dignity.

I swiftly left and walked out of the restaurant, back down the steps I had glided up just moments earlier and on to the street sobbing, my hands trembling. I reached inside my bag for my phone and went to ring my best friend, only to fully appreciate what Nigel had actually just said, Sarah of course, was no longer my best friend. Then there was the sudden realisation of the depth to their lies and the deceit over such a long period of time. My life had suddenly become an overwhelming disastrous mess, I had no one to talk to, no one, no one at all, I felt completely abandoned. The enormity of it all became too much and I felt faint and nauseous.

"Can you hear me pet? What's your name? Can you tell us your name?" I opened my eyes to see a man kneeling in front of me, my head supported by his rolled-up jacket. I felt a sudden pain as the button from his jacket became trapped in my ear. I winced as I tried to gather my thoughts. "Are you in pain? Can you tell us where the pain is? Can you point to where it hurts?" the man asked, sounding very concerned. "It's my ear," I mumbled quietly, as I pointed to my head. I heard the scream of an elderly woman as she leaned over to look at me. "Oh! My goodness, she has a fractured skull. The girl could be paralyzed," she screamed. The man next to me curtly responded, "Do stop exaggerating Gladys, it could be something quite simple. Go and sit down on the bench over there." He looked down at me and said, "the ambulance is on its way, I can hear the sirens."

To be honest, I think my worst injury was fractured pride and ruptured embarrassment. I had only fainted, yet it was causing so much fuss. My lowest point of degradation was being wheeled into the ambulance on a stretcher chair, wrapped in a bright orange blanket, it was like being carted off to an asylum in a straight jacket. By this time, a small crowd had gathered to further add to my humiliation. I heard a woman sarcastically comment on my black eyes obviously coated by the mascara from my tears "She looks like she's rehearsing for Halloween!" The paramedics however were really pleasant, particularly when I informed them afterwards of the pathetic circumstances in which I had found myself in. Once I had been thoroughly checked over, they agreed I was well enough to take a taxi home. I stepped out of the ambulance, much to the utter amazement of the growing crowd, now hungry for even more drama. I walked away, my head down to conceal my level of shame. Some members of the crowd started making nasty remarks to humiliate me even further. "Look there's nothing wrong with her." "All of this waiting around and for what? nothing?" They were like an eighteenth-century mob awaiting a hanging and purely for the sport. I had no energy left inside me to muster up an argument to counter their stupid commentaries, so I just continued my walk of shame.

Everyone always makes inappropriate comments at times such as these, comments like "time is a great healer" in an attempt to make one feel better, frustrating comments which I always thought were useless, pointless advice, however, time has actually allowed me to move on. Almost two years after that disastrous day and with a great deal of financial help from my mother, I purchased a small flat located not too far from where I worked. Desperate to leave my parental home, I moved in with my cat, Wilbur, who was the single and most significant part of my life that I received from my relationship with Nigel. Wilbur was my one and only best friend in those days, not that we didn't have our challenges! To be completely honest,

Wilbur turned out to be a "she", "she" had already been named and by the time I discovered the mistake, it was too late, so I kept the name Wilbur, convincing myself it was broadly a unisex name.

Wilbur would climb onto my bed each morning to wake me up, she didn't care what I looked like first thing in the morning and her love for me was purely unconditional.

On this particular morning I was exceptionally late and my lack of sleep from the night before, added to my total lack of energy and enthusiasm. I had so desperately needed to fuel a positive start to my day and as always, when your day starts badly, nothing at all seems to get any better. My left shoe, which had been hiding under my bed, the one I tripped over repeatedly on my way to the bathroom, was suddenly missing. I hauled the storage boxes out from underneath the bed, hoping in the magical moonlight the shoe had slithered behind the dusty boxes left undisturbed since moving into the flat. Of course, it was nowhere to be seen, so the outfit I had chosen that day, which matched the tights and the shoes, was no longer an option. A quick plan B transformed me into a black and white spotted dress, one which I hated. I bought it having seen an advert on television. It was skillfully described as "a dress for every occasion, including the office". It was on sale, expertly marketed as the *'go to dress,' the best buy outfit of the year.'* A simple belt cleverly transformed it into eveningwear, and then flat shoes and a veiled scarf, skillfully converted the whole outfit into work attire. I spent weeks waiting for the order to arrive, the outfit had sold out instantly. However, when my parcel eventually arrived, I enthusiastically tried on the outfit, it looked dreadful. It looked nothing like the pictures of the stunning six-foot, skinny model. My five and a half foot, slightly rounded frame did not do justice to the empire line design and adding a belt didn't hide my ever-expanding waistline. However, the planning that had gone into acquiring this dress meant I was going to wear it regardless. The truth was post Nigel, I had lost interest and didn't really care how I looked at work or whether I impressed anyone. I had given up trying to compete with the attractive girls in the office, in-fact I had pretty much given up on any drive for life generally. I was no longer concerned about being popular or having close friends. I found most of the girls at work boring, I had nothing in common with any of them. All they discussed was social media, certainly not one of my strongest points. I intentionally avoided social media since the breakup with Nigel; I didn't feel like broadcasting my fall from grace via Facebook. The thought of having to delete old photographs opening up to the world that I was a complete and utter fool, was too much to bear. I also got sick and tired of looking at profiles of happy people, captured in randomly posted photographs. It made me bitter and twisted, reading about their all so perfect lives. I once, accidentally, "liked" one of my ex-boyfriend's posts while loitering around his profile, and despite my desperate efforts, I couldn't undo it. The final straw was when I unfortunately accepted what appeared to be a random 'friend request' but it turned out to be some kind of porn site which continued bombarding me with adverts and bizarre invitations from so called 'perverts.' So that was it for me, no more social media, my life as a social butterfly was over before it really got started.

As I stood staring into the mirror that morning, I looked exactly as I felt, dreary, ugly, fat and boring. "You will just have to do Charlotte, you're reasonably tidy and presentable," I said to myself as I left the bedroom, only to trip over that illusive shoe I had been searching for. It was now strangely disguised in a towel, as if it had stepped up its hiding game so as to further ruin my day. 'I will not be beaten, today is positivity day!' I recited over and over in my mind as I walked to the car, mimicking precisely what it said in the positivity books. I switched on the engine and the petrol gauge said the tank was almost full. So, with a fixed grin on my face, I thanked the universe for this minor success and headed off to work.

Work was Forsett Insurance; I had been there for almost ten years in the same role, I had never been, nor ever been considered for a promotion in all that time. Plenty of somewhat pretty and more popular individuals who had joined the company subsequently, had moved with speed up the ranks, overtaking me in the process. I resigned myself to thinking this was all so superficial but hoped one day old man Ross, the C.E.O, would appreciate and recognise my hard work and dedication and elevate me to the dizzy heights of the eighth floor, where they had a water cooler and large windows overlooking the city. The catering staff only visit the eighth floor twice a day with a trolley laden with snacks, fruit and all kinds of other goodies. I often speculated if I ever made it to the eighth floor, ought I to choose the fruit, as I saunter sexily back to my desk or should I choose a huge, bulging, cream cake and drop crumbs all over my computer, while I devour it.

Well, it didn't matter at this moment because the trolley never even ventured onto the seventh floor. We all had to rely on the service of a vending machine that would keep my money and leave me waiting, in vain, for my packet of crisps or chocolate bar. The crisps repeatedly getting stuck in the machine and failing to drop into the draw below.

I would often return to my desk empty handed, only to be confronted by the annoying and most irritating Dylan, who sat at the desk closest to the machine. Dylan had only recently joined the company and he saw himself as a 'mover and a shaker,' when in reality, he was just out and out irritating! Annoyingly however, he was infuriatingly good at his job and the sheer volume of work he had attracted to the firm in just a few short weeks, had provoked reverberations of excitement on the eighth floor. Even old man Ross ventured down to the seventh floor to shake his hand, saying he wanted to put a face to the name.

Dylan had the gift of the gab and boy did he love himself, he wore chic trendy suits and consistently commented on how 'cool' he looked on a daily basis. He had dark, curly hair, short at the back and at the sides, with an annoying habit of sweeping the front of his hair to one side relentlessly. I hated the fact he would always be sitting at his desk when the vending machine had cheated me again. The highlight of his daily entertainment was watching me standing there, powerless while my crisps were suspended in midair, going nowhere. I glared at him as I walked away from the machine. Sniggering, he would lean back into his chair and place his feet up on the desk saying, "We make our own luck in this world, Charlotte."

The traffic was always dreadful in the city, particularly in the rush hour and I would spend at least twenty minutes just waiting at the repeatedly changing traffic lights, while the traffic never moved. This morning was no different, I was listening to the radio as they issued a warning that a lorry had broken down on the bridge causing a gridlock, asking everyone to avoid the area, so I resigned myself to being late. I called work and spoke to Maureen, the receptionist, explaining the extent of the traffic jams and that I had no idea what time I would arrive, pleading with her to cover for me. Her response was a simple and curt "no," a characteristic of her usual inhospitable tone, as she swiftly ended the call.

Determined not to be infected by her negativity, I persuaded myself to continue with my mantra, saying to myself today is going to be a good day. Little did I realise that today would be the day my life changed forever. At times I actually enjoyed being stuck in traffic, particularly if the music on the radio was entertaining, while I people watched. Staring at the cars parked beside me, I would try and guess if the driver was happily married and whether or not he had children. If there were two passengers, I would guess if they were a married couple or having an illicit affair. I had developed quite a skill with my speculations, it was easy really, I could pick out the married couple because most never spoke to each other during their journey. It would pass the time anyway!

I was nearly forty minutes late when I arrived at the entrance of the car park. I rummaged through my purse trying to find my barrier pass, as I pulled up at one of the two barriers. Then, just to add insult to injury, Dylan pulled up at the barrier next to me in his sporty red car and shouted, "Good morning, late again as always Charlotte?" I frowned at him as his pass lifted the barrier instantly, mine however wouldn't work at all. I was compelled to press the 'help' button and explain through the intercom system I was an employee and needed access. "Loser!" Dylan shouted, as he drove off, leaving me to breathe in the exhaust fumes left in his wake. A crackling noise came from the panel next to the help buzzer; I couldn't make out the words but assumed the voice was asking what I wanted.

"My name is Charlotte Sage; I work for Forsett insurance and my barrier pass doesn't appear to be working." A further crackled voice came from the buzzer panel, but again I couldn't understand what they were saying but assumed the barrier would lift but nothing happened. Two cars subsequently pulled up behind me and grew impatient at my predicament. Eventually frustrated with waiting, they reversed and changed lanes, having to access the opposite barrier, much to their utter disgust. I pressed the help buzzer once again, but this time received no response. I sat waiting wondering what I should do next, for what seemed like an age when an elderly gentleman in a fluorescent jacket sauntered over to the barrier. "Oh, thank god, someone who can help. I can't get my barrier pass to work," I explained in exasperation. The man didn't speak but merely nodded, so I handed him my card in the confidence he would check to see if the barrier was damaged and that my predicament was not my fault. He took the card from my hand, glanced at it, handed it straight back and informed me my gym membership had expired. Crimson from the embarrassment, I made several apologies for my stupidity as I rummaged through the depths of my bag, only to discover that I didn't have my barrier pass with me. I tried again to make my apologies, which he didn't acknowledge, however he took a card from his pocket and placed it on the card pad, lifting the barrier without uttering a single word.

I quickly turned on the car engine, desperately hoping the barrier would remain up until I had driven through. I flung my handbag onto the passenger seat trying to compose myself, determined this negativity was not going to be the order of the day, when everything fell out of my bag into the foot well on the floor, sending its contents in every direction. The top fell off my new, expensive lipstick and proceeded to roll under the front car seat as I turned the corner of the car park, I thought breathe, relax, think positive, I can pick it up later once I am parked, they're not going anywhere.

The car park was completely full as per usual. I never expect to find a space below the fourth floor, they are normally taken up by people who essentially arrive on time. I turned up onto the fifth floor only to be met by Dylan walking across the car park smirking from ear to ear as he taunted, "Up to the sixth floor for you, Charlotte the loser!" I decided to pay no attention, and I drove along the fifth floor, where I noticed two spaces next to each other at the end of a row. There was one car in front of me, there you go, my luck was changing, guaranteed a space! I patiently followed the car in front and waited courteously while they maneuvered into one of the remaining spaces. The driver was obviously struggling to reverse into the space, a problem I could easily relate to, parking was not my strong point either. She attempted to reverse into the space a number of times, when eventually the lady got out of the car and smiled at me, as she walked across the car park to the lift. I returned the smile, reminding myself of my newfound positive attitude until I discovered the front end of her car was parked overlapping the next space, leaving no room for me to park.

With the smile firmly wiped off my face, I carried on up the multi-story ramp to the tenth floor, where there was, as always, an abundance of spaces. I parked the car, then gathered the contents of my bag from the floor and re-packed my handbag. My expensive lipstick was now covered in fluff and hair and the top nowhere to be seen.

Feeling totally disheartened and my positivity starting to diminish rapidly, I headed for the door of the stairwell. As I opened the door, I heard what sounded like a woman singing, quickly followed by a mans voice saying, "I am recording you to prove you are completely tone deaf." There were no other cars in the vicinity, indeed no one else on the whole floor of the car park. The voice went quiet, I could hear nothing but the distant drone of the city traffic coming from the ground below. As I pulled the door open to climb the stairs, I heard the voice again, the same words followed by the singing. Intrigued as to where the voices were coming from, I turned back towards the car park but still saw nothing. As if on repeat I heard the same thing again. I forgot all about the fact I was already late for work and followed the source of the noise walking towards the door leading out onto the roof of the building. The door had a large safety handle with warnings all over it, advising the roof was "an at-risk area" and "not to be entered without permission."

Flouting the warnings, it took all my strength to push the handle in order to release the door, almost falling onto the roof as it flung wide open with an enormous gust of wind, flinging my body as if I was as light as a feather. I had never been onto the roof of the building and the sheer size of the area took my breath away. Huge gusts of wind swirled around me as I stood holding tightly to the door, it was weird because on the ground it was such a still, calm, warm day. The roof top was baron, the floor comprising of gridded, metal frames filled with small stones serving as some kind of drainage, it was obviously not designed for anyone wearing shoes with even the smallest heels. Very gingerly, I took a few steps out onto the roof, keeping ahold of the door as if it would, in some way, prevent a blast of wind from sweeping me across the huge expanse of roof and off over the edge.

I glanced around but couldn't see anyone or hear anything other than the dull hum of the traffic below carried on the wind. Convinced I was now hearing things, I decided I needed a coffee to set aside the calamitous morning, I needed to get on and do some work. I tried to pull the door with both hands but struggled against the sheer intensity of the wind and the weight of the door. I tried to push the door from the other side in order to close it but as I did so, I heard the voice singing again. This time the sound appeared to be coming from the vicinity of a large air vent to the right of the door, about ten feet away from the left edge of the railings. I cautiously walked over to the vent but couldn't see anyone. Then I suddenly thought the voice might have been coming up from the office windows below, carried on the wind but I quickly dismissed the idea as I remembered the windows didn't open on that level.

Acutely conscious of my fear of heights, I stepped slowly to the right of the vent and peered around the other side. I placed one hand holding on to the vent for safety and leaned over to take a further look. My hand began shaking and my knees became weak, as I caught a glimpse of a man's legs dangling over the edge of the roof top between a gap in the barrier. I slumped onto the floor, my back against the air vent as I tried to catch my breath in a state of precipitous panic. I felt nauseous, my limbs useless and heavy. I opened my mouth to try and speak but nothing came out. I felt myself starting to hyperventilate, it was as if I was undergoing an outer body experience. I tried to scream out and tell the world there was a man on the roof and he was about to jump but the words wouldn't leave my mouth. I tried to focus and concentrate on my breathing to get some kind of control but struggled even more. What seemed like minutes was, in reality, possibly only seconds, my fear was interrupted by a man's voice saying, "I know you are there, just leave me alone."

Even so, I couldn't speak, I physically couldn't reply. The man spoke again. "Are you actually alright, whoever you are?" he asked with genuine concern. The irony of this desperate man about to jump off a building and commit suicide and he was asking me if I was okay, was running around inside my head. Anxiously again he said, "Are you having a fit or something? You need to breathe normally; you sound like you are hyperventilating. You don't need to be here, just go back to where you came from." I leaned forward, unable to stand or take control of my lower limbs, when I just caught a glimpse of a fair-haired man with designer stubble. He was wearing a navy sweater with jeans and trainers, sitting quite casually with his legs dangling over the edge of the building, as if perched on a park bench. Images of this man plummeting down onto the street below, made me feel dizzy and physically sick, then out of nowhere I managed to utter the word, "sorry."

As I spoke, he turned around and stared at me, I was terrified at the thought of him moving even an inch from such a precarious position, it sent razor-sharp shooting pains all through my chest. "What are you sorry for?" he inquired. Before I could reply he asked me politely, once again to leave him alone. "I don't think I can walk. My legs won't work," I replied. "How the hell did you get onto the roof in the first place?" he asked.

I pulled myself up into a more composed seating position and continued to try and breathe slowly and deeply. Very gently I started to control my breathing, I realised I needed to call for help so I rummaged through my bag searching for my phone. As if anticipating my every move, he stated, "forget it, there is no signal on the roof, which was one of the reasons this particular place is perfect for committing suicide." So, if he decided at any point to 'bottle out' and ask for help, he couldn't change his mind and phone anyone, so the lack of signal made his decision final. I looked down at the screen on my phone, he was right, there wasn't a single bar to connect.

For a few moments we both sat in silence, the sound of the wind was deafening and really intimidating. I felt the cold wind freezing into my bones. My last-minute choice as to what to wear that morning, the outfit designed for any occasion, was obviously not for such an occasion as this!

# Chapter 2

The ability to comfort people in times of emotional need had never been my forte. Even with my best friend, I was not the best listener or the most understanding or sympathetic person. Conversing with my cat, Wilbur, was the extent of my people skills and anyway Wilbur would never answer back. My mother described me as a 'closed book' as a child, while my father said I was 'not a particularly gregarious creature.' He thoughtfully made my lack of interaction with others, sound more like a product of nature rather than a fault. What to say and when, was now at this very moment in time, at the forefront of my mind. Tact and diplomacy and being able to say the right thing, seemed essential in the situation in which I found myself right here and now.

Still unable to stand, I leaned forward to look at the man balanced precariously on the edge of the building and said the first thing that came into my mind. "Hello, I'm Charlotte, I have some mints in my bag, would you like one?" I heard the pathetic words leaving my mouth, powerless to retract them, anxiously wishing they would disappear in the sound of the enveloping winds. I steadied myself waiting for the fully justifiable response. "Would I like a mint? Fuck me, I've heard it all now! No Charlotte, I would not like a mint, I would like you to go! Shuffle your backside over to the door, maybe your legs might remember what to do when you get there. Go on, get back to your own life and let me get on with mine." I was desperately searching for the appropriate and sensible response in order to try and appease the situation, but I couldn't think, my mind clouded in the fear of what might trigger a potentially fatal reaction. There was a long pause, what on earth was he contemplating in the silence? Was he still annoyed by my ludicrous repartee, the silence became too intense, and I found myself pronouncing, "Well you won't have a life if you jump, will you?!" The man sat in silence for a few moments as if stunned by my comment. "Let me guess Charlotte, you are a detective?"

Without acknowledging his sarcasm, I found myself waffling, about how I worked in insurance dealing with small claims up to a value of five hundred pounds. My mouth started to run a marathon sales pitch, telling him most people didn't claim the excess payment of almost three hundred pounds otherwise their insurance premiums would increase, so the cases were really straightforward. He laughed, saying how insurance is a reflection of his life, there was no point in having it. For a single moment, the gravity of the circumstances escaped me, I tried to justify in my own mind, why insurance was so important, as if dealing with a prospective customer, then mid-sentence I stopped my sales pitch and started apologising.

He sat once again, in silence for a few moments

without acknowledging my pathetic statement, as if deep in thought. "You don't need to be sorry none of this is your fault, none of this is anyone's fault but my own. I'm not saying that to attract any sympathy, so please don't try and tell me it isn't my fault because the plain fact is, this is all my own doing."

I tried to think of an appropriate response but failed miserably "We all make mistakes, it can't be that bad, I mean it's not as if you have killed someone, or have you?" I asked. It was more of an assumption and a rhetorical question and I certainly didn't anticipate an answer. "I caused my wife's death, so yes I have done like you say, the worst thing possible," endorsing his right to be on that ledge.

I had images of a man putting his wife's body under the patio or the elaborate plan to cover up a murder as described on the crime investigation channel on TV. Could this man be a murderer? I could be sitting on the roof of an extremely high building with a murderer. I hadn't the faintest idea as to what a murderer looked like, but this man didn't appear to fit the profile. I didn't feel threatened in any way, despite the fact I was sitting with a stranger who had just confessed to killing his wife on the edge of a high building. It was like watching those films, when you see a young girl walking along a dark alleyway, anticipating the fate that awaits her and you think to yourself 'I wouldn't go down there.' Yet here I was on the roof with a man who had just confided in me he had caused his wife's death. I looked over at him as he sat gazing down hopelessly at the ground below. He looked exhausted and miserable, not at all threatening, with dark heavy circles around his eyes, his skin was pallid. There was a sense of despair in his words, as if he carried the weight of the world on his shoulders.

"I'll go and get help? I'm sure there is someone you can talk to about this kind of stuff. There are people who know what to say to make you feel better." I pleaded. "I'm going to jump. I don't need any help to make a decision, as you can see, I have already made it and anyway if you go for help, I will be dead before you reach your car door." I didn't know how to respond to that, I just desperately prayed in silence to any God that maybe listening, to send me a signal, just a single bar of a phone signal would do, so that I could at least text for support. I looked at my screen in the hope God was listening and focused all my energy on my phone. Not a single bar flashed back at me, signifying my own level of desperation. Unsure of what to say next I decided on the first thing that came into my head, "How long have you been sitting on the ledge?". He told me he had been there since the early hours of the morning. He said he had been into discuss a possible insurance claim with regards to his father's boat but they had refused to pay out on the claim. He had returned to his car and found himself sitting there considering his options until at least sunrise. "You're not going to kill yourself over an insurance claim?" I blurted out petrified that my employers were responsible for placing him on the ledge.

"No, I just called in for my father, his claim has been going on for months, they were most unhelpful and found every excuse in the book not to pay out. I think that it was the last straw really. When I got back to the car, I couldn't bring myself to turn on the engine, so I just sat there. I saw the security guard go in and out of the roof top door earlier this morning and thought now was as good a time as any. I thought why not? Why not here? So here I am," he answered as if there was some form of logic in what he said.

"If you were to change your mind, I could ask the insurance company to review your father's claim if you like. I can assure you they are very reasonable and if a claim seems unfair, old man Ross takes a personal interest in ensuring it's resolved." He laughed with an air of cynicism and said, "Fair! whoever said that anything in life is fair?" He reached into his pocket for his phone and proceeded to play a video of a woman singing while a male was talking. It was the singing I had heard earlier I recognised the male voice as his. "Is that your wife singing?" I enquired. "Yeah, that was my wife, Grace. She isn't my wife anymore, well, she isn't anything now really," he said as he placed his phone down on the ledge next to him.

"How long has she been gone?" He shook his head saying, "Why do people use the words 'gone and past' is it because 'dead' is too hard to say, let alone to live with?" Then he paused for a moment, "Well she's been dead now for a grand total of eighteen months and three days." I wasn't really sure why I asked such a question the truth is time was as irrelevant to me as it was to him.

"Do you have any other family apart from your father?" I asked. "Yeah, both my parents are around as well as a happily married sister who happens to be married to another woman and they have two children together. The kids are beautiful, born by sperm donors, organised through some website. I was totally against it all at first but thankfully it turned out to be safe and legit, they have two handsome boys. All very unconventional, I know but that's life nowadays." "Your mother's heart will break if you jump," I said, as if he had not thought of that already. He paused for a while and said, "My mother's heart is already broken. Her heart broke at the same time as mine and she has watched me slowly die inside ever since. My wife's death tortures her as much as it tortures me, at least this will be some kind of closure and she could move on with her life." "Of course, it won't end her torture, don't be so ridiculous, she will live with it for the rest of her life because on top of everything else, she will have lost her son!" I snapped. He didn't answer or even turn to look at me.

I felt the wind pick up, gusting its chill throughout every bone in my body, making me shiver uncontrollably, depicting the unfriendly reality of nature. There was a long silence but strangely enough not an uncomfortable one. "Suicide doesn't end suffering, it just passes it on like a baton in a relay race," I said, as if I had some kind of insight and understanding of such issues. The truth was I remembered reading the exact words scribbled on a poster in graffiti at a bus stop. "Did you read that on the back of a cereal packet?" he asked without turning his head to look at me, clearly pointing out my response was simply empty words without any real knowledge. I couldn't lie, "well, yes actually I did read it but isn't that how we all learn?" "I don't know Charlotte, is that how we learn useful phrases which may one day come in useful?" he answered mockingly. He sat quietly and shivered as the cold wind encircled him.

"Aren't you freezing? The wind is really bitter up here?" I asked. Images of a sudden strong gust of wind blowing him over the edge crossed my mind. My stomach flipped at the thought of that high ledge overlooking the ground below. "Yea, I'm cold but I think I'm mostly numb now because it doesn't feel as bitter as it did earlier," he answered calmly. "Are you not scared the wind may blow you over?" Another of my stupid questions, which I regretted asking as soon as I had said it. He paused for a while and then spoke as if he had drawn the response from his boots. "I'm scared of everything Charlotte, just looking down at the ground below makes me feel sick, ironically enough I'm petrified of heights. You know what? I honestly think I'm just as scared of living as I am of dying. If the wind did take me, it would be a blessing because right now at this moment in time, I haven't got the balls to jump or not to jump. I'm stuck as if in limbo, but I think it's hell."

There was a long pause as though he had run out of things to say, then as if he was remembering the good times in his life he said, "She loved the sky, the moon, the stars, sunset, sunrise, all of it. Everything around us she saw the beauty in it all, something I never appreciated until she pointed it out. She would come home from work and ask, "Did you see how beautiful and bright the moon is this evening?" And I would reply, "Yeah, beautiful." She knew very well I hadn't even looked up at the sky. Strangely enough, when the sun rose this morning, I felt the closest I had ever done since she died, it was as if she enveloped me in the daylight. Just for a second, I thought I could hear her voice in the wind," he was smiling as he mimed her very words. I could see him re-living their moment in time over and over in his mind.

He didn't speak for a while, lost in his thoughts while I attempted to shuffle myself further towards him so I could see him, without leaning over the edge. I could see this desperately unhappy man, his despair almost palpable, his grief utterly profound it, was all so very sad. With the sound of the busy morning traffic unnervingly carried in the wind, I peered down at the ground beneath where everyone was going about their daily business, they resembled ants scurrying about in all directions, totally oblivious as to what was going on above them. I tried frantically to think of any suitable things to say, the plan in the back of my mind was if I could keep him talking, eventually someone would look up and notice him and bring help. I'm sure that's what I have seen them do on television. I had watched programs where especially trained individuals were called in to say all the right things and talk the "jumper" down but I right here and now, couldn't think of anything to say that might help in the slightest.

The noise of sirens could be heard in the distance and for a second my heart jumped. "They're not coming for me or providing a net in which to catch me, if that's what you're thinking. There's a fire on the wasteland right over there, that's where they are going." He pointed towards a disused factory across the other side of the city where clouds of smoke were floating into the atmosphere. Unfortunately, he was right. "Would you like a safety net?" I asked but received no answer. I asked again. "I mean any kind of safety net such as support or counselling or anything?" "I have been seeing a councillor since Grace was diagnosed. They said it would help me deal with my 'anger issues.'

During my last session she pointed out I had been receiving their support for months and asked how I felt it was going? That is code for, 'we cannot do anything else for you.' As I was about to leave, the councillor was asked to take a phone call and left the room leaving my notes on the desk and I read them. I looked at the first page, which was the demographics and diagnosis information. Apparently, I went from grieving to becoming depressed three months ago. Ha! when do you do that? and how do they know when you move from one to the other? Does that mean my grieving time is over? Is there a set time you are permitted to grieve?"

"Did therapy not help at all?" I asked.

"I think it did at first because I wanted to die with Grace there and then, on that bed. I begged any God who would listen to take me with her. She knew that too and so made me promise to go on living, and in her own way she kept me going. My promise to her is my reason to get up every morning and live some kind of existence. I often think the only reason I carried on living was my promise to her and it's become more difficult to keep as each day passes. Like everything, everyone's sympathy runs out after a while. You get the usual advice from friends, tips on how to 'move on.' Thing is I don't want to move on, I want to be dead and be with Grace. She was my life, there is nothing else for me in this life, I have no purpose on this earth.

She is still my life and until the day they took her body away I didn't realise I would be left with such a huge cavity in my life, one so large I could fall into it and never be able to climb out. I miss her so much it physically hurts, the pain racks through my body. The thing is, I welcome the pain because in some strange way it takes away the pain inside my head, even if it's for a short time. The pain is not like any other pain, it's extremely intense, the most overwhelming pain you could ever begin to imagine. A penetrating ache which takes over your whole body and mind, and with it the most incredible desire to see them again, to touch them, just talk to them once more, otherwise you feel you might explode.

My mother once said grief is an overwhelming love that no longer has a place to go and I am starting to agree with her. I'm ashamed to say I even started to 'self-harm.' It's not with the intention of hurting myself, it's basically the feeling of release while inflicting the cut, I feel as though I am about to burst if I don't do it. The worst part of it all is, I had zero respect for people who self-harmed, I believed them to be feeble attention-seekers. Now I am that pathetic man I detest. In the height of summer, I sit in a long-sleeved t-shirt so my mother can't see the scars, making excuses I'm cold in twenty-five-degree sunshine. I cannot go swimming without revealing the scars of shame, how embarrassing. However, I continue to do it because I am a pitiful man. When I go to the support groups I ought to introduce myself as "I am Jacob, I am a pathetic man."

"I was going to ask you your name," I have been sitting on this roof with you for quite some time now and I didn't even know your name." "I think we kinda skipped the formalities, it's Jacob, my name is Jacob Ashton." He raised his head and bellowed, "My name is Jacob, I am a pathetic widow who lost his wife to cancer." He paused for a moment and said, "I've said that so many times in the support sessions, they said it would allow me to start releasing the pain but it hasn't, I still feel every inch of that pain. It hasn't gone away; it has just turned me into Jacob who attends support groups with his pain." As he was speaking I noticed he pulled the sleeves of his jumper down over his hands, now acknowledging the cold. "Are you married Charlotte?" he asked. I was slightly taken aback by his question and had to think for a second because I had actually forgotten.

"No, I'm not married, I live in a flat in Woodbridge by the sea with Wilbur, my cat. I used to be in a relationship with someone, but it turned out he was having an affair with my best friend and decided to leave me because they are having a baby together." "Well, that is shit, isn't it? Sounds like you're probably well rid of him." "That is what everyone says but I don't feel it, not yet anyway, I'm hoping time will heal my scars but until then I have my cat." The conversation went quiet again while the wind seemed to be diminishing, leaving a sense of calm on the rooftop. "You really don't have to sit with me Charlotte, although it's very kind of you," he said as if the silence had caused him some unease.

"I can't leave you Jacob, I know I'm not very good at saying the right things, I can't leave you." There was another awkward silence between us. "Did you say Grace died of cancer? You said earlier she had been diagnosed but you also said her death was your fault, so how could that be possible?" I said, feeling slightly intrusive. "She did and it was but it's a long story," he replied. "Well, I'm all ears, it may pass the time while we're both sitting here. I would like to try and understand what brought you to this miserable place."

# Chapter 3

It was all so surreal, sitting there waiting for his next move with a feeling of total and absolute lack of control over the whole situation. Jacob's ashen, solemn expression revealed his inner sense of hopelessness, apparently overshadowing many of the good things that must have happened in his lifetime. As a stranger, I could see his life improving but his despair clouded his view of any possibility for any future. I genuinely wanted to understand what had brought him to this point of despair and had asked the question, not really expecting to get a response. The exhaustion and all-encompassing pain and grief seemed to make him feel he was a burden on others, his friends and family he felt were better off without him. I wondered what he was thinking sitting there? Was this his cry for help or just a demonstration to the world of just how much he was hurting?

The silence was almost deafening, compounded by the whistling of the wind as it swept through the murky caverns of the parking lot. Thick, dark clouds gathered in the sky above us, creating a dark, heavy blanket ready to engulf the pair of us. The atmosphere: damp with the fine rain gusting around the skyline. I grabbed my dress pulling it down over my knees to try and protect myself but with little effect. Once again I broke the silence "Of course, You don't have to talk to me, I mean it's not as though I am trained or anything like that. We could always talk about something else, something completely different if you like?." I paused awkwardly and then came my classic one liner "How about this weather? isn't it awful?" I immediately put my fist in my mouth and found myself needing to apologise, promising faithfully to have my tongue removed. Under normal circumstances I often open my mouth without thinking and put my foot in it. Jacob remained silent, not responding to anything I said, it was as though he hadn't heard my ludicrous comments, he seemed to be miles away, disassociated by his thoughts. "Can you even hear me in this wind?" I shouted, but no reply was forth coming. "I didn't mean to upset you, by expecting you to talk about something so awful, personal and intimate, honestly I didn't." Then the silence was broken, "I remember when I first met Grace, we were at a friend's party." I saw a glimmer of a smile as he remembered that evening. "It was certainly not love at first sight, well Grace wasn't my usual type, the bright red, wild hair and a personality to match, she always stood out in a crowd with her freckly face and her enormous bright smile. Her clothes reflected her personality with her individual fifties style tailoring." He chuckled as he described how she would buy dresses from quirky designer shops, her zany individual look often turned heads wherever she went, although her dress sense was not to everyone's liking."

"She was totally altruistic, such a generous and caring

individual. That night at the party, I had gone upstairs to use the bathroom, only to find an intoxicated Grace being sick over the toilet. I apologised for the intrusion, closing the door swiftly. I waited outside on the door but she didn't venture out, so I knocked on the door to see if she was okay. I had no idea why, but I decided to stay with her, she had been drinking far too much, so I held her hair back while she continued to throw up. I remember she was slumped on the bathroom floor and she looked up at me in her drunken stupor and pointed out that I looked very drab in my light blue shirt and jeans; it caught me completely off guard. When she felt slightly better I walked her home, I had no intention of staying but from that evening onwards I never left."

"She had a way of making shitty days feel good." He paused deep in thought while I sat and waited. "She didn't have a professional career type job as such, she worked on a busy coffee stall on Market Street. Everyone knew her, she had the art of making people feel special, she always took the time to chat to all her customers, and they loved her. She was good with money; she could literally save from nothing. She used to up style old furniture and sell it at the local market on Milner Lane, on a friend's stall. Any money she made went straight into the teapot on the shelf which she kept for travelling, discovering new places, something she loved to do."

He had quite obviously placed her on a pedestal, one so

high she was beyond his reach. A part of me felt envious, no one had ever done that to me. Sitting on the roof freezing in a skimpy dress put a whole new perspective to my life and I found myself looking at the world through someone else's eyes. At the very thought of her, his eyes lit up, she was everything to him I could see that it was something we all strive for in a partnership. Even the cold chill of the wind that blew right through me could not match the cold emptiness I felt in my heart. I spent years trying to be someone's Grace, failing miserably. Here I was listening to his despair, and anger as well as loneliness, hoping to reduce the emotional burden enough for him to want to carry on living.

"You know what Charlotte; I fell in love with her very soul, her thirst for enjoying life and all it has to offer. She made me feel whole, and together we were complete. We had three happy years doing the things young couples dreamed of. We travelled to exotic places, staying in the best of hotels, we even bought a small, quaint house on the edge of the city and renovated it. Grace was so talented she turned an empty shell of house into a home. She had the log burner installed just in time for the autumn, making our little home into a sanctuary, the best money we ever spent. Evenings lying in front of the log fire making memories to last a lifetime.

I felt an overwhelming desire to compete with Grace

and her talents, so I tried frantically scanning my brain to recall some impressive journeys in my life and my abilities as a homemaker. I struggled to conjure up images of me back packing around India, with braided hair and a youthful carefree life but figment of my imagination was all it truthfully was, I've never travelled. The truth is, even in my so-called happy relationship, I lived a lie and being a perfect partner was never a realistic or achievable goal. The only attempt at clearing out my life was decluttering my wardrobe which was pathetic to boast about. My selfish thoughts had taken me away, albeit briefly, from doing the only helpful thing I was capable of and that was listening. Thankfully, Jacob hadn't noticed my temporary lapse in attentiveness, he continued resurrecting his memories, while looking out across the distant rooftops of the town, seemingly oblivious to the definitive death drop below him.

Jacob continued recalling his memories "Grace would even make plans for our retirement; we were going to sell up and buy a houseboat to live on, so we could travel around the country on the canals and waterways. I remember she wanted geraniums to line the starboard of the boat, with the picturesque ideology of cruising the river, stopping for breakfast or the occasional pint along the way. I was totally and utterly taken in with everything she intended to do and looked forward to sailing alongside her." He spoke about her with such sentiment and passion, for a few short moments I felt as if I had known her once upon a time. "Do you have any children?" I asked. He threw his head back laughing sarcastically. "Oh, to be blessed with children. No, no, we didn't have any children. Grace would say good things only happen to good people, well good things don't happen to bad people and I'm rotten to the core." I wished I hadn't asked, I appeared to be rubbing salt into his glaringly open wounds. "How about you Charlotte, do you have any children?" he asked, genuinely interested to know. "No, I don't have children, I would like to, maybe one day. I think I would struggle with the "looking after" side that comes with children. Even the cat has to remind me to feed him! My mother says I'm leaving it too late and I would already be classed as a 'geriatric' mum now at twenty-four. She exaggerates a little but I do get where she is coming from." He sat quietly as if pondering my reply and comparing it to his own life.

"Grace never really wanted children; it was me who wanted children in our relationship. She used to say, if it was meant to happen, then it will." She was always open to the idea of adoption but I wouldn't even discuss it." Jacob cupped his head in his hands, as if unable to face his own emotions saying, "If only I could go back and reconsidered that option now."

"Grace had no family of her own she had grown up in foster care with no desire to track down her parents once she was eighteen. She talked about her foster mother with kindness, an elderly lady called Rose who took good care of her, but sadly she died when Grace was only sixteen. She was devastated at the time apparently, she said it was like losing her real mother, she felt privileged to have known her." she said.

As usual, the words leaked out from my mouth before my brain was able to engage and prevent them from being spoken out loud. "I had a friend at school who was fostered, it was literally a living nightmare. Grace was really lucky to have found someone who loved her. My friend spent the majority of her teenage years grounded and like so many teenagers when she was eventually allowed out, she rebelled and started smoking, clubbing and drinking. Her foster parents were getting paid shed loads of money to care for her, so technically it was a job, so perhaps they ought to have had more patience, considering her background and not having her real mum." I continued to blurt out my idiotic views, as if it was from the ideology of a fifteen-year-old justifying everyone's' tolerance of her disruptive behaviour, until I remembered she actually grew up to be very loved individual and very successful in her professional life, mostly thanks to her foster parents.

"Grace was never a wild child she was content. She lived by the mantra that you have to make good of what you are given otherwise things can never get better. She loved Rose and felt very loved by her. They shared a love of fifties fashion and renovating old things. She saw the beauty in everything where others failed to. Some people search for a lifetime to be as content as she was but to her it came naturally." He paused for a moment, picked up his phone and played a recording of her singing. He allowed it to play up until his voice was heard on the recording. "Why could I never let her be so content? I pressed her into thinking she should want for more, more drive, and for what? I was so selfish." "She sounds like a really nice person," I replied. He smiled. "She just had this way about her she put people at their ease. She was so sincere, everything about her was pure. I should have known when we met she was too good for me. Beautiful people like Grace never last long, do they? I deserve all the misery I get."

# Chapter 4

The wind started to get a little stronger now and I felt so very cold. As I looked over at Jacob, I could actually see the hair on the back of his neck standing on end. I sat back into the shelter of the air-vent which took the brunt of the gusts of wind but where Jacob was seated, he was fully exposed to the icy blasts. I had visions of him developing hyperthermia and not being able to think straight and consequently falling. I felt a desperate need to keep him talking, as if it were my duty to buy him some time.

"I don't see how you are to blame for Grace's death. Cancer is terrible but it's totally indiscriminate, you had no control over that?" Jacob sighed deeply, "They never said as much but I know it was the I.V.F that made the cancer grow. She was healthy before we started the course of treatment and had bundles of energy. Funny, I always thought if we had a baby she was better suited to parenthood than me, she never needed much sleep and was always active. I secretly dreaded the inevitable sleepless nights and counted on her liveliness to pull me through. Going through all the various treatments made her ill, I know it did. The doctors denied it, obviously but they would, wouldn't they?" He directed the question towards me as if in someway I had some answers for him. I stuttered as I tried to think of a logical answer.

"I don't know much about IVF, in fact very little but I am sure if that was a risk you would have been warned about it. I know it's not an easy process, I have friends who have been through it and they really struggled. "It's an agonising process which challenges true love in any relationship and we were no match for it," he answered, with hints of anger in his voice. "You can't force anyone into undertaking something like that, I'm sure she understood the risks and the consequences of what she was doing but I'm sure she was just as determined to see it through as you were." Attempting to provide some sense of clarity to his self-blame. "The cancer may well have happened independently of the treatment you know. One reads all the time about people who do everything right in life, they don't drink, don't smoke, but still get cancer, even kids get it, it's totally indiscriminate. My mother, I remember once told me about an elderly neighbour smoked enough cigarettes to kill three men in his lifetime and he lived until he was ninety-eight. While my poor grandmother died at seventy with cancer and she never smoked a cigarette in her life." But it seemed my words of reassurance were wasted on Jacob.

"It was completely my fault, making her mess about with her body like that. I forced her into it, I was the one who wanted a baby so badly. I was utterly selfish and now I'm paying the price." He spoke quite openly about how, trying to conceive naturally, was fun at first, the sex was passionate and exciting. But time took its toll as the months went by, no pregnancy and the enthusiasm soon faded. The advice the doctors gave was to invest in an ovulation kit and have targeted sex on the right days and this became their plan B.

"God! That testing kit was the worst thing ever. It was performance on demand. I can't believe I'm even saying this but sex very quickly became a chore. They should print a warning notice on the box 'can damage your relationship.' The passionate, sexy Grace had gone but I let her go without realising the importance of what I was losing. Sex for us used to be such fun; we would laugh and talk afterwards, eat food, watched films then have sex again and again. We enjoyed our time together but as Grace lay with her legs up on a pillow for twenty minutes, the passion was quickly lost. She didn't have a perfect figure and I'm certainly no body builder but we loved each other, including our imperfections, which made our relationship so perfect. I gave it all up and replaced it with a testing kit!"

Genuinely curious I asked the obvious question, "Why didn't you do something about it, instead of feeling like that and saying nothing. I mean why does that happen in relationships? People moan about what they have at home and then go out and find what they think they are missing in someone else, as if the grass is greener on the other side. Well, I can tell you the grass is just as brown and patchy on the other side, it just looks greener from a distance?" I knew I was referring my life and the brown, patchy, grass people often leave behind, hoping for an answer from someone who had no idea of the underlying meaning, how I felt or indeed what I wanted.

Jacob turned around and looked at me with total disbelief in what I was saying "I have no idea why you are talking about grass but in answer to your question, I have no idea why I didn't do anything and deal with it all at the time. Life just got in the way, as it always does, blindsiding us from what is really important and God help me that was so important. Grace knew it and tried to face it. I knew it and chose to just whine and complain rather than dealing with it, as I do with everything in my life."

She even rang me at work one day, to tell me the kit we nicknamed 'the oracle' indicated it was the perfect time. Perfect times had been few and far between recently. Despite the mounting pressure at work, I made my excuses and left the office n a rush to get home. When I arrived, Grace was waiting in the bedroom, no sexy clothes, no excitement or romance, just sitting waiting for the next stage in the process. As I walked into the bedroom she took one look at the expression on my face, stood up and got dressed. She put her coat on and said, "Come on, we're going out!" That chilly afternoon we walked along the canal, we enjoyed the feel of the "ocean and getting caught in the rain" we enjoyed drinking hot chocolate rather than "the taste of champagne" as the song lyrics go and we talked about everything but babies. It was the best afternoon in a long time. I sometimes walk along that same canal hoping I might find her there."

Jacob sat quietly as the noise of the traffic appeared to soften for a moment and we both sat with our own thoughts. Suddenly Jacob leaned back from the ledge, I thought he was going to slip over and drop to the ground below, my heart jumped missing a beat. "Could I have a mint?" he asked. Thankfully, I took the mints from my bag and passed the packet along the ledge towards him, so they were within his reach. He leaned over and stretched his arm to grab hold of them. The mint felt like the proverbial life belt to a drowning man, I felt quite emotional at the fact he had asked me for something I could actually give him. Maybe from that moment there was a connection between us, albeit for a few moments, maybe he might listen and I could help him. As he opened the mint he said, "That day as we walked along the canal, Grace said "this isn't more important than us and what we have together." Of course, she summed it all up in one sentence but it still didn't go through my selfish, thick skull."

During the next few months, we both agreed not to completely give up on the idea of having a baby and decided to seek help from the specialists. Friends had become pregnant through IVF and when they told us about their experiences it seemed a more controlled way of going through the process and perhaps in some small way, transferred our burden into the hands of doctors. The procedure wasn't quick or cheap and commanded a huge financial commitment from both of us. We made a pact to look out for each other and if one of us started to lose faith, we would pick each other up."

He continued to talk about the weeks of tests and counselling which followed. Grace endured numerous invasive and undignified procedures, while Jacob was apparently left in a cubicle with porn magazines and a white, plastic pot while nurses waited outside. "The results indicated I was fine but Grace was not producing healthy eggs." Jacob paused, and then said "Perhaps we should have stopped then and there, as it was at this point the pressure moved firmly onto Grace's shoulders. It became her vocation in life, it was as though she needed to prove something I'm not sure to whom, either to me, herself or the world, I don't know but it became all consuming. Our daily routine was dictated by a set timetable of copious injections which she had to self-administer. I tried a few times to help but left her with bruises and so I wouldn't do it anymore. I kept apologising for her bruises each time I saw them, I was happy when they finally healed.

Then came the implanting of the eggs which was dependent on increasing the number of injections, up to twenty a day. While Grace never complained, I always knew she wasn't too happy interfering with the natural processes within her body but I know she went along with it for my sake. The joy of making our family complete made the experience more tolerable. The overriding ambition of ultimately having a baby one day, overshadowed everything else in its wake and perhaps we didn't appreciate how much we were both sacrificing, particularly financially. Costs were inevitable but we hadn't really given them a second thought." Jacob recalled their quarrels when Grace said having a baby was in the hands of greater powers than doctors. Jacob was, it seems, annoyed and frustrated at her remark and snapped back, "I'll remember that when I empty our bank account to pay the bills from the clinic next time. I am working a million hours of overtime to pay for this shit which you don't seem to have any faith in. I came out with it in sheer frustration, exhaustion and anger. I did apologise but like all cutting words they left their mark." He said in his defence.

He spoke in some detail how Grace managed her disappointments better than he did, she would go out for long walks on her own. Her selflessness was evident throughout the whole process. He noticed she cried a lot during this time and spend hours in the bath, topping up the warm water, she was there for hours. Her appetite changed, as did her weight, which subsequently affected her choice as to what she would wear, there were less of the jazzy, bright clothes he was used to seeing her in, all so unlike her traditional style.

Life became a "more need than want" basis and it obviously had taken its toll on them both.

Jacob continued talking about the treatment process and as the date approached for the implant, he said it felt as though all their efforts were soon to be rewarded. He explained that throughout the procedure, he held on tightly to Grace's hand, promising it would all be worthwhile. He described how he felt their intimacy started to return. This was a journey they had decided to undertake together and this was their reward. It was all very clinical, they had two fertilized eggs so as to increase the chances of a successful pregnancy. Jacob said he felt somewhat awkward but was encouraged to actively support Grace. Once the eggs had been implanted the consultant shook Jacob's hand and said, "Congratulations Dad!"

I saw Jacob looking out across the buildings illuminated by the morning sky and as he looked up and said, "Those words cemented everything, it was worth every sacrifice we had made along the way. Afterwards we left for home on a colossal high, one that neither of us had ever experienced before. I handled Grace with the fragility of glass, while she lay in bed with her feet up on a pillow, waiting on her hand and foot. She would eat only the food she had discovered helped during pregnancy and she remained calm throughout.

Of course, neither of us could truly relax but we both

did a good impression of pretending to each other that we were, even though we both knew deep down we weren't. The worst thing about the whole process was the fact once the eggs had been implanted then we were officially pregnant, left in the hope the pregnancy would remain stable and the baby allowed to grow." Jacob beamed as he remembered Grace couldn't stop smiling at the thought that at that very moment, she was pregnant and proudly carrying our first, precious child. He said it seemed each time he looked at her, she was cradling her stomach as if in the first forty-eight hours of being pregnant she could externally protect and comfort her baby. Jacob then said it was three weeks before they truly started to believe their baby was real. It was still early days but he said they started to talk like parents: making plans, they dared to dream.

I found myself briefly touching my tummy, as if in maternal support of his sentiments for his baby. The notion of motherhood washed over me like a warm wave. I always thought parenting would come easily to me and at the perfect time, in my daydreams of a perfect relationship but it was still a distant ideology. Motherhood held a mixture of emotions for me of love and guilt, feelings so utterly overwhelming I certainly couldn't face them right now. I questioned the inevitability of life, everyone had problems but despite them, we perceive ourselves to be so alone in our turmoil. I was intrigued in listening to his tale of joy but soon it became apparent he too had consequences to his experiences. "We were nine weeks into the pregnancy" Jacob continued "we were quietly confident, we both walked around with happy smiles on our faces as if we were hiding the best kept secret in the world. We would often look at each other smiling and laughing without saying a word. You know what, Charlotte?" Jacob chuckled "my father even started tracing our family tree, somehow it suddenly was important to understand and appreciate our extended family links, family had become everything."

"I decided to buy Grace a present on my way home from work, something that extra bit special. I went to one of those fashionable chocolate shops close to where I worked and carefully selected 12 chocolates, boxed and tied with a huge bow. There were hundreds of chocolates to choose from, each coated with individual pictures or letters representing a poignant memory from the donor. The twelve pictures I chose told the story of our life together, the last chocolate coated with a picture of a baby with a pink and blue heart. I made my journey home excited to see Grace's reaction to her gift, only to discover our future happiness shattered into a thousand pieces. Grace was crying in the bath cradling a large glass of wine. She didn't have to say a word, in fact she didn't have to speak at all, her face said it all. I was devastated and couldn't find the words at that precise moment, words of sympathy or the standard 'We can always try again,' seemed totally inadequate. I slid down onto the bathroom floor and sat with her while she cried. I would like to think I was some support but the truth is, I was a selfish bastard because as she sat crying, I kept on wondering whether or not this was her fault. This resentment started to grow inside me, like a tumour.

Grace needed to go to hospital based on the clinic's advice to ensure the foetus had come away safely. I made my excuses when I dropped her off at the hospital, telling her I couldn't stay because of work commitments. She said, she was fine and completely understood but she knew I was lying to her; we both knew she was giving me the proverbial 'hall pass.' That evening I went for a walk through the park, it was raining, I got soaked. I walked around and around feeling sorry for myself, not really giving Grace a second thought. I thought she would naturally cope because she always coped with everything and anything on this journey so far." Jacob went quiet, he appeared to be gazing over the rooftops across the town, immersed in his reflections of what had come to pass.

At that moment I felt obliged to stand up for Grace and take the feminist high ground, so I asked him why he had chosen to lie to Grace and not explain to her how he felt. She would have understood and come to terms with the situation. I offered him no opportunity to defend himself, I started ranting about how men had always lied to me, leading my life in all kinds of directions, directions I never wanted to go. I held myself up as a martyr to the decisions of men. Jacob didn't respond with the comprehensive answer I really wanted to hear. I hoped he would confirm I was right; that I had been vulnerable and manipulated in all the decisions made during my life, but he didn't. He just sat quietly and said nothing because really there was nothing to say. I found myself answering my own challenging questions in his uncomfortable and deafening silence.

I was contemplating my own life, it is like the perfect storm, everyone is better off with hindsight. The sad truth is hindsight is exactly what it says on the tin, understanding the event after it has happened. No matter how hard we try, it is impossible for us to change the misfortunes of our past and regrettably we don't appear to learn from such misgivings, even though we like to blame them. During her darkest days, I always remember my mother saying we either get up and get on with life or we drag our past along with us like a heavy chain around our necks. I certainly drag my heavy train around with me and I honestly believe Grace liked to get on with her life, despite carrying her own heavy chains weighing her down.

Jacob broke the silence and smiled as he started talking about Grace again, "You know Charlotte, despite everything, within three or four-days Grace was back on her feet and going about life as though nothing had happened. Unfortunately, however, we both made the crucial mistake of not mentioning our baby. I suppose it was more for my benefit, I refused to be drawn into any conversation on the matter and avoided the subject entirely. Ha! I remember my mother and Grace were in the kitchen, I overheard my mother telling her that men survive heartbreaks on their own and she gave my father as an example. I felt this irresistible desire to rush in and scream, *I didn't want to cope at all* but I decided to hold back on that, I'm that predictable male, I said absolutely nothing."

"Within a few months without any real debate, we were booked into the clinic again for our second round of treatment. D-day was now a mixture of fear and pleasure. We waited like inmates on death row, expecting the worst rather than hoping for the best. Grace said this time she didn't feel pregnant, I just told her it was nerves. It wasn't nerves, she started losing the baby during the early hours of the next morning.

We contacted the clinic and told to 'double up' on the injections, it sounded so simple but suppressed a mass of unforeseeable obstacles. The amount of hormone Grace was injecting made her feel ill. The bright yellow plastic bin we had been given for disposing of the needles, was at the point of overflowing, despite the instructions on the side of the tub stating to fill up to a maximum of two thirds full, then empty. The refrigerator housed numerous boxes of medication, all lined up in date order with the time at which they were to be administered. On top of which and maybe the greatest obstacle of all, was the doubling up on the medication, which meant thousands of pounds added to the existing bills we were already struggling to pay. We had maxed every credit card available, I spent hours moving debt around from one card to another to ensure we got interest free credit wherever possible. We borrowed from the bank and family members in the hope, once the baby was born, the debt would seem like a small price to pay. The truth was the finances weighed heavily on both of us and placed a noose around our necks." "Tell me about it!" the words came straight out just like that, my mouth engaged itself. "I manage finances about as successfully as the titanic managed their lifeboats." Jacob grinned at my flippant comment.

Jacob carried on, "Despite our trepidation we continued doubling up on the injections each day. Grace was covered in bruises and ached from head to toe, it was horrible to see her like that, she would cry at the drop of a hat. The treatment process was like a never-ending web we were weaving with no end in sight, once you start you have to keep going otherwise everything you are sacrificing becomes worthless. We knew our efforts were all in vain when Grace started once again, to lose our baby. This time no tears or drunken baths; we were both just utterly miserable and starting to accept the reality this was not going to work."

I could only try to imagine the traumatic reality of what Jacob was describing and said "It's all so very sad, but you never really know anything for certain. Some couples spend an absolute fortune and continue for years with IVF. It must be like taking a ride on a never-ending rollercoaster and it becomes impossible to jump off. No one wants to stop on a low when the best high may well be just around the corner. I cannot begin to imagine the level of personal and emotional pressure you were under; Grace's hormones must have been all over the place. You want to see me when I'm hormonal, honestly, I can't even choose a cake in the cake shop window without turning into a nervous wreck and collapsing into floods of tears."

"I don't know Charlotte; it was all getting too much and the doctor suggested we both take some time out before trying again. I have no idea why but without hesitation almost instinctively; we both shook our heads and said our intention was to carry on with at least one more final attempt. Our relationship from that moment became extremely challenging. We were both under a great deal of pressure and the last thing on our mind was sex, in reality sex was non-existent, there was no fun or excitement in our daily lives, we simply existed and worked. There was no physical intimacy, in fact that all faded away. I think we needed to protect ourselves from each other in some kind of bizarre way. However, I did remember thinking, at this rate we would have no relationship at all in which to bring up a child. I'm a coward, I never really felt brave enough to say it out loud."

"Two of our close friends had started their own families around this time. One couple had applied to adopt and were waiting nervously with an empty photo frame on the fireplace, ready to display a picture of their soon to be son. Another couple were heavily pregnant with their first baby, which happened without any of the interventions we had endured, I found myself avoiding the "social get togethers," I ought to have been happy to be a part of."

"Although Grace courageously attended them all, with beautiful gifts for each of them and allowing herself to be genuinely happy for them. I have to say Grace wasn't selfish and bitter like me, she did what everyone ought to do; she carried on with her life, patiently hauling me along with her, hoping perhaps one day I would let go of my self-pity, I couldn't find it in me Charlotte, I couldn't. I became increasingly more insular, isolating myself from our friends and as a result pushing Grace away too." I saw the devastation and frustration in Jacob's face. I watched this man, wallowing in his own self-pity, he was thinking of no one but himself and his inner most feelings, I decided this time I would hold on to my words and remain silent.

The look on his face at that moment, reminded me of

Nigel, my ex and the pathetic look he had on his face when I walked into the restaurant, the evening he annihilated my life in all but a few seconds. I felt that same anger flare up inside me and found myself wanting to despise Jacob for his selfish, self-centered attitude. His decision to commit suicide, somehow appeared justified in view of the egotistical mistakes he had made. But deep down I knew nothing could ever justify the darkest places that open the window to suicide. I wanted to know more about how he had arrived in such a desolate place, a place I could not possibly begin to comprehend. Unaware of my inner sentiments he continued his story.

"It was another four weeks until D-day arrived for the third time. We both greeted the occasion with very little, if any of the enthusiasm of the first time, both too scared to raise our hopes, only to be devastated once again. Grace went to the clinic with my mother this time, who constantly made excuses for my selfishness in not going. I started to spend more time at work, avoiding the inevitability of going home and facing Grace. I found every opportunity to point out when I did get home, that I was the one working all hours earning the money for her treatment. We handled the pregnancy with more of an indifference and the attitude, if it works it works, if not then so be it. I think Grace was silently hopeful but concealed her feelings, possibly to protect me from further disappointment.

Following the treatment, we went about our daily lives as if nothing out of the ordinary was happening. I started to play badminton after work, as a distraction from the daily mundane routine of life. I started to drink quite heavily in the evenings, as if I had the sole right to drown my sorrows instead of focusing on hope. Grace was so patient; she endured my temperamental outbursts of self-pity and she cleared away the empty wine bottles without comment. I knew she was concerned because I knew how much she loved me. She always kept trying to encourage the slightest glimmer of positivity in me, she even used the last of her savings to buy me a badminton racket and a kitbag when I announced I was going to play to get fit. There was a racket sitting on the kitchen table, waiting for me when I got up one morning. Grace had already left for work and it was freezing cold outside. There was a card attached to the racket that simply said, "I love you, enjoy G x." I suddenly felt a tsunami of guilt as I read her words.

I decided to take her scarf to the coffee stall where she worked, knowing she would be cold and as I approached the stall I could hear her chatting away to her customers. She always had the friendliest manner when she was speaking to them. I stood back listening to her for a while. She always found a common rapport with each and everyone she spoke to, offering them hot coffees and hot chocolate with her cold, fingerless, gloved hands. I remember when she embroidered those gloves with the flowers, she said it was a talking point for people to engage them in conversation. The back of her gloves resembled bunches of wild cotton flowers she had sewn individually. She once told me an elderly gentleman at the stall had said the daisy was his wife's favourite flower, on seeing Grace's gloves he said it was a sign she was still with him. After that Grace added even more flowers to make people smile.

While I watched her from a distance, in a single moment I believe I fell in love with her all over again. Her hair was unruly, falling out of the two braids on each side of her shoulders. Her cheeks were red from the cold, her lips dry from the heat coming from the boiler. She had a smile for everyone, including me. She was surprised to see me standing there holding her scarf. She moved across to the side door of the cabin, kissed me and then told me to hurry up and get to work, because I was running late. "Wait," she said as I turned to leave, she passed me a milky coffee and a large chocolate cookie in a paper bag, kissed me again as she ushered me on my way. I felt a warm feeling inside, not just from the warm drink. She could do that in one kiss, she could put me back on track and let me know I belonged. That day was a turning point for both of us. Slowly but surely, we made an effort to have more time for each other, and as the weeks went by everything appeared less stressful.

It was a few weeks before I truly came to my senses, it

was during a game of badminton with Alex from our account's office. I realised I had been so busy avoiding the realities of life, it was passing me by. Alex randomly said, "Third time lucky?" referring to his winning shot, it was an epiphany, was this third time lucky and my wake-up call? Life suddenly felt like a runaway train I was running to catch. Following the game, I raced home to find Grace sitting on the sofa in her dressing gown with a towel wrapped around her head like a turban. As I hurried to take my coat off and unable to get my breath I stammered, "We are still having a baby, aren't we?" She giggled, "Yes we are but we are having supper first."

I cannot remember a time in my life when I felt so complete and deliriously happy. That evening we talked as if we had just found each other, having been separated for years. I held her bump, which was now quite prominent and we dared to laugh about suggested names for the baby, some we hated, then trying to agree on names we both loved. "Charles," we both said at the same time in a random, slightly telepathic way. It was decided there and then despite not knowing the sex of the baby, if it was a boy, then Charles it was." I interrupted "Baby names I always thought would be a hard one for me. You always relate names to people you know, don't you? I don't know a Charles but I know a Charlie. He was a dreadful person, people do say there is a lot in a name, don't they?" I babbled. Jacob turned to look at me in utter disbelief "Charles is

Charlie. How can you not know that is the same name?" he snapped.

"Well obviously I know it is the same name, I was merely trying to point out it was a shortened version of the name and therefore seemed different," I was struggling to redeem myself. "I just pointed out that I would find it difficult to decide a name, that's all. There's no need to be so rude," I said sternly. "Well, it wasn't difficult at all!" Jacob snapped.

There was an awkward pause until Jacob once again, started talking about the months of misery they had endured. "The stress only started to disappear when life presented us with a whole new set of problems, this time pleasurable ones. We both became more relaxed as the pregnancy progressed and I even began to go on nights out with friends who were now new parents. They were full of advice on a whole range of issues, school catchment areas being the hottest topic. I laughed at them, pointing out we were only six months into the pregnancy and if school was a problem, we would face that further down the line. I was quickly put in my place, and informed names need to be reserved for the best schools from birth, in fact it was more of a priority than applying for the birth certificate these days.

Grace would smile listening to the debates; confident she would handle these problems when they arrived.

She started to go shopping, buying little white vests and sleep suits, I was amazed at the size of them, with visions of our son trying to fill them. There were tiny pairs of baby socks rolled into a ball, barely the size of an egg which made me smile. Grace commented how the first size nappies were the same size as those she used on her first doll as a child. Furniture and new clothes slowly started to fill our home, ready for our new addition, nothing would ever be the same again, two were soon to be three and everything in our lives would change to accommodate our new family.

Conversations had a sense of anticipation and excitement, planning for a future we only dared hope for, these shared dreams brought us closer together. Evenings on the sofa no longer meant sitting at opposite ends focused on a mobile phone, now we would cuddle each other, we laughed, life was good, very good, looking forward to our future together. I suggested I should cancel my golf membership; it was really expensive and I hardly played. I thought that when the baby arrived, I would have less time to play but when I mentioned this to Grace she said, typical Grace, "But you love golf and you waited so long to be enrolled as a member, you would miss going. You don't need to stop playing when Charlie grows up, he can go with you." Her answer made me laugh, I realised everything in life was changing and changing for the better.

# Chapter 5

Grace was almost eight months pregnant, she was exhausted, she thrived on comments from strangers who would say she was blossoming. We had taken photos at every stage of our growing bump. Every picture reflected a glowing, proud Grace cradling her bump comforting 'him' while he was growing inside her. She would take videos of her stomach moving around as the baby kicked and she would send them to me at work. The most recent picture taken of 'Charlie bump' was my screen saver on my computer at work, a picture which greeted me every morning when I arrived at work.

I was sitting at my computer one morning updating my calendar, adding time out for paternity leave, it made me smile just typing it into the computer. I texted Grace to tell her my time off for 'nappy duties' was all booked in with an emoji of a smiley face and a baby at the end. Her reply came back quickly saying the 'Charlie bump' had been very quiet today and must have been tired from all the kicking the evening before. I replied telling her to have a warm drink to get him moving again. Feeling totally contented, I responded to my outstanding emails and got up from my desk to make a coffee. I was chatting to one of the girls in the office, who had herself just returned from maternity leave, I often made a beeline for her to pick up practical information not necessarily available in the baby books.

Then came the news that nightmares are made of. Rhona, one of the staff, came rushing into the kitchen babbling something about an urgent call, I needed to go straight to the hospital. She thrust my keys and my coat into my hand and escorted me to the lift, explaining Grace was on her way to the hospital in an ambulance. The journey across the car park seemed to take an eternity as I darted around frantically looking for the car. I couldn't think straight, my head was pounding, my mind racing, I found myself trying various doors of white cars, thinking they were mine.

The sluggish pace of the traffic was so frustrating, I found myself praying for the red traffic lights to change faster. I could hear ambulance sirens in the distance and wondered if it was Grace, I feared the worst. A journey which usually takes ten minutes was now into twenty-five as I drove through the City Centre. I could hear the sound of my message tone on my mobile over and over again calling to me from my jacket pocket lying on the back seat, where I had thrown it in haste. I found myself pleading with drivers in front of me to move more quickly, as if in some way they could hear me. I eventually arrived at the hospital and ran across the car park, ignoring the ticket attendant as he shouted at me that I needed to pay and display in order to park. The two most important things in my life were under threat, so the idea of a parking ticket had no right to a space inside my head at this moment in time. I remember thinking how anyone could be so trivial.

I arrived at reception to be met by my father who took me to a waiting room. I asked him about Grace and the baby, he said the doctors were saying nothing, they were with her carrying out some tests. My mother sat outside the ward crying but stood up to hug me as I arrived. My father prized her away, telling her I needed to be with Grace. He patted me on the back as I knocked and entered the room, saying to myself the immortal words, "be strong, son."

That afternoon I think Grace cried herself to exhaustion when we were informed by the doctor our baby no longer had a heartbeat. She cried desperately trying to explain she could still feel the baby moving, they must be mistaken. She tried to negotiate with the doctors to give her time as she explained the bump often went still for periods of time, perhaps he was lying in a funny position so his heart could not be heard. We were told there would be a further scan that afternoon followed by an induced delivery. We held hands and our breath as the sonographer glided through the gel on Grace's stomach. We gasped in anticipation each time we heard noises but were told it was the blood flow and not the heartbeat we desperately longed to hear. The sonographer discreetly turned the sound down to prevent us from any further false hope. At one point she turned the screen away and clicked as though she was measuring the foetus, while smiling apologetically as she watched us having to endure the process. She left the room making her apologies, she returned shortly afterwards saying the doctor would see us in the Oasis Suite and in the meantime to have a cup of tea.

We waited needing answers, Grace's hands never stopped cradling her stomach, she wanted to hold onto every last minute with our son. The consultant walked in with half a smile on his face and shook my hand. He sat on the edge of a chair leaning forward, as if what he was going to say needed him to be close. He explained the results of the scan, there were some abnormalities in Grace's cervix and ovaries. The word 'abnormalities' is never a good word to hear in medical terms and it threw us both a curve ball, we had only expected to hear why we had lost our baby. He went on to change the word abnormalities and refer to 'a mass' attempting to explain in layman's terms that the baby's umbilical cord had been damaged by this mass and had prevented the blood supply from reaching the foetus. Our heads were spinning trying to take in all the information, like candy floss twisting onto its stick. Our heads were spinning so fast churning out questions, which generated further questions. We were both drowning in an abyss of questions in fear and grief.

We were told the first step would be for the baby to be delivered that afternoon and then tomorrow Grace would be seen by a Gynecologist; a specialist in this particular area. By this time, we had exhausted our list of questions and were both in a daze. Grace was taken to the delivery suite and pumped full of pain killer drugs to make the labour as smooth as possible.

I found myself wondering around the corridors of the hospital, flinching each time a door opened and a nurse walked out talking, not knowing was the worst. I was lost and felt utterly powerless; it was as though the earth was giving way beneath my feet, like quick sand. I waited for what seemed like an eternity when a nurse came and ushered me into the room, at the same time, dressing me in a white gown, a reminder of the clinical standpoint of the situation. I walked in, desperate to see Grace who would somehow make everything all right but I was met with a tired, broken Grace who needed me to be strong for her. However later that evening my life lost all direction and spun completely out of control, like a tornado in a field of wheat, everything took on momentum. They delivered our beautiful son Charlie, weighing four pounds and six ounces. He was taken to a crib, cleaned and wrapped in a blanket. They handed us our son, the most precious gift, his tiny face was a picture of perfection. I was overwhelmed, his tiny fingernails, his hands the size of my fingertips, I was stunned. I felt an instantaneous love, something I cannot put into words, we knew he was no longer with us; he was stillborn.

We stayed with him for the rest of the following day, holding him, speaking to him, telling him stories and singing quietly to him. We knew our time with him was limited, which made each moment all the more precious. It was like being in limbo, he wasn't breathing, yet for those few precious moments he was there with us, it was just like he was sleeping. We took turns cuddling him, even timing each other in equal shares. Grace changed him into a small, blue baby grow and a hand knitted, blue cardigan with blue, train shaped buttons. He was sleeping so peacefully, so much so, at times I was convinced I could see his chest move, as if he was breathing. He was beyond perfect. He had fine, dark hair slightly thicker on the top of his face. Grace commented on how beautiful his dark hair and long eyelashes were. His skin was pale and delicate, like porcelain, which made his hair look even darker in comparison. We held his hands, everything about him was totally perfect. In the short time we were with him it almost felt as if he were alive in the midst of us.

A woman came into the room and apologised for disturbing us, explaining she was from the special bereavement team and asked if we would like to take a print of Charlie's hands and feet as a keepsake. We had mixed emotions about the whole thing but with a strange kind of pride, like parents who watched their baby have their first photograph taken, we decided to go ahead. Grace took off his little sock and pulled up his sleeve so as to not get ink on his clothes. The intense emotions around this seemingly normal activity in this kind of setting became unbearable. Grace wiped his little hand and foot afterwards and dressed him. She wrapped him in his blanket and cuddled him as if he would need pacifying after this ordeal. I looked at her and I swear my heart shattered, as I watched her being his mum.

At eight that evening the nurse came to take Charlie away, Grace wrapped him in a blanket put on his hat and kissed him as the tears rolled uncontrollably down her face. I had never felt pain like that in my entire life. It was physically hurting; it was as if my heart was being torn from my chest and that little boy had taken both our hearts with him. A massive part of me died that day the very moment he left the room.  Grace instructed the nurse to take good care of him and to cuddle him, she said he liked to be cuddled. The nurse nodded as though she fully understood she was holding the most precious baby ever to be born. The nurse had tears in her eyes, she was trying not to blink to prevent her tears from escaping and stop her from doing her job. Her tearful eyes were comforting and will stay with me forever.

Grace cried herself to sleep that night as family cautiously and apprehensively looked in on her, cried and then left. Flowers arrived, bouquet after bouquet to such an extent the nurses started to spread them around the ward for purely practical reasons. In the early hours of the morning Grace was awoken by the nurses who gave her a blood transfusion, they regularly checked on her, updating observations records and writing up her charts. By nine the next morning the room was a hive of activity when Grace was rushed off for a scan. The doctor said there was some internal bleeding and they needed to know the cause. Everything after that happened so fast, the results of the scan highlighted a need for immediate surgery and Grace was rushed away before we had time to discuss anything." I could see the tears in Jacob's eyes, it was all so very sad. I was so engrossed in his story I felt the despair and devastation, as if I was there in the moment. "What happened Jacob, did Grace have some kind of infection? Lots of women get infections at times like that." He didn't hear nor did he answer my question. His mind had drifted to re-living every detail as he told his story.

"I paced up and down the hospital corridors unable to tolerate the confines of the ward. I bought a packet of cigarettes and walked outside into the grounds to smoke, even though I hadn't smoked since I was a teenager. An elderly man sat at the opposite end of the bench, trying to piece together a vaping cigarette machine with little success. Without saying a word, I handed him a cigarette and a lighter, he nodded as he accepted them. We were both in our own world of despair, blowing smoke into the air.

"She doesn't like me smoking, the wife. She bought me this vaping thing but I can never get the bloody thing to work," he said, as he placed the pieces inside his pocket. "She is dying, my wife and I have not got a bloody clue what I will do without her. People are not given to us forever, are they? They are lent to us for however long they are meant to stay and that is it," he said as he got up and left. I didn't answer I simply nodded. We were both strolling through our own hell and nothing I could say would change the direction of our journey.

Grace came back from surgery about three hours later, she looked so pale and her eyes sunken and dark. The sheets on the bed were fresh and the baby case she had brought with her had been discretely removed by my father under my mother's instructions. "Smoking won't help," my mother said as I entered the room. My Father loved to smoke a pipe but had been forced to give up. My Mother fluffed up the pillows and tidied the bedside table, picking off petals which had dropped off in the intense heat of the hospital room. A nurse popped her head around the door to explain the surgeon had been called into another emergency but would discuss the procedure as soon as he had the opportunity. "There you go everything went well, now we just need Grace to come home and we can get her better. People are better looked after in their own homes," Mother said with a sense of reassurance. "How do you know everything went well? We know fuck all. We know Charlie is dead and Grace is ill, that is what we know," I shouted at my mother as if in someway she was to blame. My father ushered her out of the room, as she burst into tears. Grace, apologising for my outburst reminded everyone emotions were running high and that we all needed a good night's sleep.

The surgeon arrived late than evening, looking exhausted. He sat us down and explained that the mass in Grace's ovary had grown too big and there was a risk of perforation. They had removed some of the growth and sent samples to the laboratory for testing, so we needed to wait for the results to decide the next stage. I shook his hand and thanked him, unable to really put into words my gratitude for his skill and dedication.

It was three days later when, a very tired Grace, was allowed to come home. The family had removed the nursery furniture in an attempt to be sensitive. The baby clothes we had bought had been bagged up and stored away in case they prompted a reminder of Charlie and caused further upset. It was as if he never existed. Grace went straight to bed, saying nothing as she passed the spare room glancing at the obvious absence of our once happy dream.

She hardly left the bedroom for days. My mother cooked and cleaned as if she were an invisible maid everything was spotless and nothing was left for Grace to do but grieve. My mother knew that was the only thing she could do to help. She had my father changing light bulbs and doing the odd jobs I had avoided for some time. She would scold him, reminding him to work quietly, as Grace needed rest and peace and quiet. She seemed to think of everything. Grace wore nothing but pyjamas right up until the morning of the funeral. My mother washed a simple black dress and left it ironed and hanging on the door next to my suit.

Hot croissants and jam were prepared for breakfast, with a note begging me to eat something and orders to try and encourage Grace to eat in preparation for a long day. She was so well organised and practically minded it didn't occur to me it was the day she was to bury her grandson." "You realise Jacob if you go ahead and jump your mother will also endure the pain of burying her son," I pointed out the obvious and waited for the response, as I followed it up with, "No one should have to bury their child. Burying anyone is just horrendous." There was a pause for a while, neither of us spoke nor indeed wanted to. The bitter wind became more cutting, sinking deep into my bones while I sat on the rooftop.

A random thought came into my head. "It was bitter the day we buried my father. I remembered thinking I was so cold standing at the grave and hoped he didn't feel cold in his coffin. It's bizarre how the mind works and what grief does to each of us? I struggled at the wake as the tears of the mourner's soon disappeared afterwards and people drank, ate and were chatting, as if at a party. My mother said people had their own way of dealing with their grief and that wakes were a celebration of life. To this day I still don't really understand, I suppose it brings people together like any other occasion and people together are stronger."

Jacob said, "Charlie's funeral was a small family affair, held in the chapel of rest at the hospital. No death is easy but the death of a child is always more traumatic and harder to cope with. It doesn't fall into the natural order of life and seems a far greater theft to those whom it affects. The bereavement teams at the hospital were extremely professional; they planned everything with minimal input from either of us. They planned things with such sensitivity knowing we were in no place to make such difficult decisions. The whole thing seemed to pass by in a mix of tears and pain. One of Grace's friends had made a blanket for Charlie, knitted in cream and swathed in flowers, with a fold at the top to place around his tiny head. Grace insisted he was wrapped in it to keep him warm, "Wrap him tight so he feels cuddled" she pleaded. "He loves to be cuddled and needs to be kept warm," she explained, unaware her logic was one of complete and utter grief and devastation.

The point of a funeral is the final goodbye and as the vicar said, "the celebration of a life however short." I could find no place in my heart for any recognition of thanks. I was angry with God, angry at everyone. I hurt so badly I wanted everyone to know just how bad the hurt felt. I tried so hard to be strong but when it came to kissing him for the very last time, I felt as if I had been stabbed in the heart. The strength went from my legs as I slumped into the chair, I couldn't let him go. Grace wept hysterically; I could hear her begging me to let him go when the priest tried to take him away from me in his tiny wicker coffin. My cries of devastation resonated around the chapel through the priest's microphone, echoing from the crevices in each corner of the chapel to the horror of the mourners. Grace's screams were a background noise in my head. The ache in my heart for Charlie was overwhelming. The pain of never being able to hold my son ever again in this lifetime was unbearable, I felt as if my soul had been ripped from my body and I was powerless to prevent it from leaving. They were taking our little boy away from us. He was ours to love, not to be taken by strangers. Nothing was making any sense, I felt like I was about to explode with pure anger and frustration. I could hear my mother trying to comfort Grace and my father telling me to be strong. I couldn't understand or follow what he was saying, it was all such a blur. My father's voice resonated around inside my head, half of me grateful he was resolute, doing what was necessary and the other half wanting everyone to know we were travelling to hell and back.

Charlie's tiny coffin was taken from me and placed on a plinth. The curtain closed as the organ played a rendition of Somewhere over the Rainbow. Prayers were said and I watched as quite a few of the congregation wept. I remember wondering if they were crying for Charlie or for us. What I do know is that a part of our souls died that day to be with him forever. So, is this what it is to be a parent? I never truly understood until the day he arrived in our lives; you give your children a piece of your heart you can never take back. I saw it in my own mother's face at the funeral, I could see her heart was breaking for me, she would take on all my hurt in an instant, something parents always wish to do. Everything that happens to your own children, happens to you as parents and the only thing you can do is to somehow try and make everything better.

Everyone was really supportive, we had such wonderful family and friends, they all tried their utmost to help but sometimes all the help in the world cannot pull you out of that huge black hole that you don't really want to leave. We had left our home only a few days before, happy excited and full of hope for the future and returned home to a life full of desolation and anguish. The fridge was full of fresh food and ready-made lasagna, labelled with full heating instructions. Everyone tried to help wherever they could, but the real truth is you don't care about the little trivial things anymore they become meaningless in the absence of hope.

Over the following weeks our lives centered around doctor's appointments and treatment plans. The mundane but busy schedule seemed to excuse us from talking about Charlie; his death became the resident elephant in every room. My parents took the dog to stay with them as a temporary measure, thinking we had enough to focus on, with Grace's recovery and grief. In the first few days, being at home, I missed the dog and thought it would have been a good idea for Grace to have him in the house particularly while she was awake. However, she remained in bed and would cry herself to sleep, unable to face anyone or life itself."

"Oh Jacob! Who on earth would be able to face anything after all that? I struggle with small everyday things. I remember I once got a letter from my doctor having had a routine smear test saying I needed to contact the surgery regarding my results. Can you believe I got the letter on the Friday night after work? By Monday morning I was wearing black and writing my epitaph and then it turned out there was nothing wrong with me." I saw Jacob's face; he wasn't amused at my effort to make light of the situation.

He chose to ignore my comments and started discussing Grace's surprise birthday meal the family had organised. He said, "The affair was to be kept low key, at her favourite restaurant. Grace tried so very hard to make an effort, she dressed in a red flowered, fifties style dress and red headscarf, tied as a band around her head. She looked desperately sad as she sat at her dressing table applying her make up. There was none of the usual background music playing while she got dressed and none of her usual jovial chit chat. She managed a smile as she caught a glimpse of me standing in the doorway but the smile no longer came from her eyes. It was a mask she now wore sending the message she was okay in the hope it would stop people asking her the dreaded question. 'How are you feeling?' There were obviously two answers, the first she was heart broken and the second one, which we use to make others feel better the 'I'm fine.'

She appeared genuinely pleased to see her friends. Some of them; bursting into tears from the sheer sentiment of seeing each other in such circumstances. There were lots of hugs and every effort made not to show too much sympathy, remembering the meal was meant to be a celebration. Inevitably once the wine started flowing the conversation turned to Charlie. Grace appeared comfortable talking about him and described him in great detail to her friends. They were all attentive as if they were broody women at a baby shower.

"Would you like to see a picture of him?" Grace asked, the whole table fell silent in response to her question. She didn't wait for an answer but proceeded to take her phone out of her bag and click onto her photographs. The atmosphere around the table became extremely tense as everyone anticipated pictures of a stillborn baby. Grace clicked onto her favourite picture of Charlie in his little blue hat and with pride she handed the phone over to her friend Meryl. Meryl leapt to her feet bawling at the fleeting glance of the picture and hurriedly left the table stating she couldn't cope with the sight of a dead baby.

The meal as you can imagine came to an abrupt end following the outburst and as the waiter came over with the birthday cake covered in lighted candles, he was quickly led away by my mother. Grace took it badly and announced to everyone she was tired, so we left making our sincere apologies. Since that evening, in the weeks to come, the exhaustion persisted, Grace no longer had enough energy to even dress herself. I'm not sure of how much of this was down to her grief or how much to her sickness, so we decided to make an appointment with the doctor. I wasn't particularly concerned at this time; my mother had said it was sure to be anemia and how common it was following pregnancy. She reached her diagnosis by identifying Grace was showing all the signs of anemia, looking pale and feeling exhausted. She said a bottle of iron tablets would have her feeling better in no time at all and after all she had been through, it was bound to have an effect. This couldn't have been further from the truth and in the days that followed the doctor's visits included frequent blood samples, scans and diagnostics by consultants.

# Chapter 6

"Cancer," that was the only word I heard uttered by the consultant from across his desk. Every word following that was a blur, the word floated around inside my head with no place to land. "Was it the mass that killed our baby?" Grace asked. The nurse and the doctor glanced over at each other as if they needed a non-verbal queue on permission to answer. The doctor sat forward in his chair with his hands clasped together over his knees. He was fidgeting in his seat, obviously uncomfortable with the whole conversation. I looked at him empathising, thinking even after all those years of training he had the worst job in the world. Studying for years to hand out to people their death sentences. "The mass would have made the pregnancy impossible to progress any further," he said with complete conviction. I watched Grace she didn't cry but thanked him for his honesty. Perhaps until that moment she blamed herself and in some way his statement may have lifted a part of her guilt. "Grace The cancer isn't curable," the doctor said in such a sympathetic respectful way. Everything went quiet and although I could see their mouths moving, I couldn't hear any words. The silence in the room was strangely deafening and hurt my head like a precipitous headache.

The Macmillan nurse took Grace's hand during the consultation and asked if she had understood what had been said? She nodded in agreement.

I sat numb, feeling unable to say anything to anyone I heard nothing other than the word cancer. I looked at Grace, her eyes were red and blood shot as she listened to the consultant's advice. He handed her booklets of information no one would never want to read in their lifetime but use as your bible in times of such desperation. Called back into the real world, I heard Grace ask, "How long do I have to live." The enormity of the question she had so bravely asked aloud was too much for my heart to take. The stark reality of it all overwhelmed me. Everything went into slow motion as we awaited his answer. I could feel my heart pounding in my chest as if it was going to burst at any second. My mouth, dry with fear, as I grasped her hand tightly, the weight of the words that followed were suffocating. I could feel Grace's hand turn cold. I looked at her face as she stared at the consultant knowing her life hung in the balance. Her face was pale, her eyes filled with tears. The consultant leaned forward expressing his heart felt sympathies for our predicament as he said, "Weeks to months depending on your response to your treatment."

He continued speaking after that bombshell, explaining about palliative treatment and a care plan. None of that information filtered through to either of us as we sat in a fog of confusion, despair and disbelief. I could feel myself inside screaming at him, telling him he must have made a terrible mistake. I was screaming inside; the pain was physically unbearable. Grace and the

Macmillan Nurse tried to calm me down as I started hyperventilating and eventually the consultation was stopped. We were both led out of the consultant's office, Grace could hardly stand and had to be supported by one of the nursing staff. I remember us leaving the hospital together, like zombies clutching at a mountain of leaflets. I have no idea how I managed to drive home that day nor any recollection of what was said, if anything, during the journey home.

That evening we lay in bed clutching each other sobbing. We talked about who we should contact but neither of us felt we could repeat the prognosis to anyone. Saying it out loud made it seem far too real and didn't fit with our present capacity of denial. We googled, 'wrong diagnosis' and found hundreds of cases where doctors had provided a misdiagnosis. It provided us with a glimmer of hope but we both knew, deep down, the reality of it all.

I have no idea what time we fell asleep that night, both fully dressed lying on the bed but the next morning I awoke to find Grace had disappeared. Blurry eyed, with an intense headache I got up and headed for the kitchen. Grace stood at the cooker dancing to the music on the radio dressed in a fifties style, spotted, red dress with old-fashioned curlers in her hair. She asked if I would like breakfast, as if yesterday had just been a bad nightmare. I tried to remind her of the reality but she quickly stopped me. She said whatever will be, will be but until then she was alive. Her defiance was immense leaving me with no room for debate. She handed me a bacon sandwich and put her coat on to go out to work.

"Work? Really? I asked. She replied quite curtly "I will say this only once and no more. Do not question my decisions, I'm carrying on the only way I know how and the only way I can possibly cope. My life is not over yet and I refuse to waste another minute of it crying and wondering about fairness and the what if's. I'm here and alive that is a fact, so that is enough for me. If I can get through one hour at a time I see that as a win win situation, so let's leave it at that. Yes, I'm going to work and I'll bring you a cookie home." With that she left, setting the bar for bravery so high I couldn't even see it, let alone reach it."

Grace continued working for several weeks, despite numerous appointments for chemotherapy and blood tests. Work seemed to be the stabilising factor in both our lives. Family and friends rallied round and did their utmost but to be perfectly honest they were as lost as we were, once they knew the circumstances. We tended to make our excuses and steer clear of social occasions, it was often all too emotional. Even routine every day normal conversations were difficult at times. No one felt able to talk about their future plans in front of us, and it often became awkward and uncomfortable. People who did speak to us spent most of their time apologising for saying the wrong thing; even the simplest of conversations became difficult.

My mother called at the house one particular day and as usual straight away went to put the kettle on. "I bet your dying for a cup of tea" she said and then burst into tears apologising repeatedly for her choice of words. Grace and my mother cried together in each other's arms; it seemed a bit of a release for both of them. I stood back and watched them go from sobbing to laughing and hugging, as if they were on some emotional roller coaster. The range of emotions ended with the obligatory cup of tea that Grace stated was 'to die for' as she sipped it, which made them both burst into fits of laughter once again.

# Chapter 7

I sat listening attentively to Jacob, utterly enthralled in his poignant story, so much so the freezing temperature of the wind on the roof appeared to have diminished. I had forgotten we were not having a typical chit chat conversation, and nothing I could ever imagine saying would even came close to the strength of emotion emerging from Jacob's narrative when I announced, "My father often said laughter is the best form of medicine," as if believing this thread of common ground may connect us both in some tenuous way. "Your father was a wise man," Jacob replied. I replied "I'm not sure if he was wise, not really. I just remember he was a pleasant man and I suppose he did laugh a lot." "You are talking about him in the past tense, did he die?" Jacob asked. I paused for a few moments reminiscing on my own past. I felt sad as well as guilty because I had stopped thinking about him as much these days. "He died in a car crash when I was thirteen. It's not something our family talk about much because some find it hard to forgive him." "You've intrigued me now. Forgiven him for what, was he a dreadful father?" Jacob enquired. "No not at all, in-fact the total opposite. He was a brilliant father and an even better husband, or so we thought. When he died, he was in the car with another woman, she died too. Initially it was thought it was my mother but thankfully it wasn't."

Jacob was surprised, "So he was having an affair?" he

asked. "Not exactly an affair, it all came out soon after the accident, he had a whole alternative life, another family in Ireland in a little town called Corkickle. My mother was devastated and apparently so were his other family. Shortly after we found out about this other family, I went over to track them down to Ireland, alone. It was a pretty brave thing for me to do, I had never been anywhere abroad before. I soon discovered it was a big mistake, I got lost on the way over and spent two hundred pounds just to get back to my hotel, only to fly home the very next day. I have never travelled alone since it was my worst nightmare. That's probably why I'm still single!"

Jacob hardly knew what to say. "I hated my father while I was growing up for all the hurt he had caused but I suppose looking back now I can appreciate how difficult relationships can be, so I feel a little different. Some small part of me admires him for managing to keep two families happy when I can't even keep a single man in my life." Jacob began to laugh out loud. I felt slightly annoyed and said, "I'm pleased you find it funny." Jacob tried apologising through his laughter but couldn't stop himself.

"My mother warned me at the tender age of sixteen to 'stay single' because the women in the family were doomed to failure when it came to love. She told me her great grandmother had fallen in love with a Lord of the manor and he was going to leave his family and all his wealth to be with her forever. The story goes that on the very day he left he was trampled by a horse and killed instantly, leaving her penniless and pregnant.

Jacob laughed even louder at my story, I was even more annoyed by his response and told him in no uncertain terms this was no fairy story but true-life family history. My anger made him laugh even louder. "If you don't stop laughing, I'll push you off that ledge," but he just laughed even louder. He laughed so much, tears ran down his face, his laughter became so infectious that despite my anger I too started to laugh. We chatted about how bizarre the whole situation while wiping away our tears. "I haven't laughed so much in a long, long time," Jacob said. "Well, I'm pleased my terrible background has cheered you up," I noted with a touch of sarcasm.

"You should write your autobiography Charlotte, it would be hilarious, indeed a best seller, you have such a unique view of the world," Jacob said meaningfully. "I don't think people would be interested in my life it's too boring. You know what? I have never left this country and travelled abroad, apart from my disastrous trip to Ireland, of course?"

"What? Never?" Jacob asked and I shook my head cementing his disbelief. "Grace loved to travel; we went all over. She always found the most unusual places, mostly off the beaten track and away from tourists. The last place we visited together was Scotland. The family clubbed together and surprised us with a short break. We travelled first class on the train to Edinburgh, where we spent our first night. It wasn't easy organizing everything as we had to plan the trip around Grace's chemotherapy to make sure she was well enough to travel."

"We stayed in a beautiful hotel, high up and close to the castle. Grace was amazed by the attention to detail of the decoration at the hotel. The wooden paneled walls and the antique furniture, it was her ideal venue. I remember how she threw herself onto the cushion-covered bed, as if she had just fallen onto a cloud. She said she had never slept in a bed with a roof before, it was just stunning. I remember her lying there gazing up at the tapestry ceiling of the bed frame. "I bet that's a haven for spiders," I said teasing her but she didn't care.

We ate that afternoon in the hotel restaurant. The food was excellent but Grace hardly managed to eat anything. The management kept apologising and offering alternatives concerned there was something wrong with the food as her plates were returned to the kitchen untouched. She felt guilty the chef may think it was his cooking, so she quietly told the waiter that it was her chemotherapy and the food was, indeed, lovely (especially the homemade warm chocolate orange cookies which arrived with the coffee.) The waiter smiled sympathetically and reassured her he would of course, inform the chef and not to worry about upsetting him.

That evening we decided to go for a walk in the cool brisk Edinburgh air wrapped up in coats, hats and gloves. We set off only stopping to peek in the antique shops with their windows full of a myriad of valuables. Since Grace's diagnosis, material things no longer held any value. Material things are forever and we knew we were not, being together was the most important thing. We took photographs and laughed as we stood listening to the sound of a band playing the bagpipes. We wandered past the busy shops taking in all the sites, people watching and then stopping for a drink in a small coffee shop so that Grace could rest.

There was every type of cake and pastry displayed in the window and the shelves were swathed in tiny, twinkling lights. There was an open fire at the other side of the bar, so we sat down in the two armchairs to take in the warmth of its glow. We watched the world go by and for a moment cancer was the last thing we had in the forefront of our minds. We sat observing the passersby trying to guess what they did for a living and laughing at the sheer random nature of our answers.

Casually sipping her hot chocolate topped with creamy marsh mellows, Grace suddenly announced. "When I'm no longer here I want you to promise me you will do this with someone you will eventually grow to really love in the future?" A lump stuck in my throat and my tears were hell bent on escaping. I couldn't turn my head towards her or even respond to her question.

She was insistent "Look at me, Jacob? This is not meant to be a sad moment, I need to know you will continue to live a full life, it means everything to me. I don't want you sulking las though you are the only widower in town. No one will ever want you if you mope all the time." I couldn't answer, I didn't want to talk about when she had gone, life without her was a place in my mind I couldn't ever face opening the door to. However, determined to keep up the positivity I said, "I am eyeing up the talent as we speak. Her, over there with the cream coat and boots, looks like she could keep me in a manner I could easily become accustomed to." Grace laughed out loud, "She is far too high maintenance for you. You're more the lady over there." Grace pointed to an elderly lady who was rummaging through her wheel along, tartan bag. We carried on laughing until the early darkness of the winter evening drew in. The lights in the café window sparkled against the raindrops starting to fall outside, signalling it was time for us to return to our hotel. Getting cold was the last thing we needed for Grace. We wrapped up and headed back up the precipitous street to the hotel. I held her knitted, flowered, gloved hand as we walked slowly back.

We took a short cut through a passageway that led to the side door of our hotel. On the landing of the first flight of stairs a homeless man was asleep in a sleeping bag on top of a large, flattened cardboard box.

Grace grabbed my hand as I tried to walk straight past. I took a deep breath at the inconvenience of her delay and reluctantly took two pounds from my pocket which I handed to her. Grace rolled her eyes at me and took the money. As he was asleep, she carefully put the money close to his hand so he would find it when he woke up. A cold drink had been spilt on the floor and was leaking across onto the cardboard where he lay. Grace took a tissue from her pocket and blotted up the drink to stop it from reaching him. The man woke up in a daze, realised what she had done and thanked her.

Grace was upset at his predicament as we walked away. "I know what you are going to say but giving money actually keeps people on the streets," I told her, confident in my knowledge. "That doesn't mean it's okay to do nothing. Did you see him? He was a young boy? I wonder what happened in his life for him to end up sleeping outside in the freezing cold?" she asked. "I don't know, it's choices people make in life, I guess." I could see Grace's mind working overtime, a look of anger crept across her face. "Bullshit! Life is hard sometimes and but for the grace of God goes anyone. All the philosophical arguments of what to do for the best is on another level and debated forever but tonight that poor boy is freezing. We walked past dismissing him on the way to our warm, posh hotel room. It's wrong, all wrong."

That was it, typical Grace! our return journey to the hotel turned into a trip to the outdoor warehouse to buy coats and sleeping bags. We bought toiletries and thick socks, we bought anything that Grace thought would help soften the burden of sleeping rough. Laden with carrier bags, we returned to the stairwell to find nothing but the large piece of wet cardboard, the only evidence anyone had been there. Grace started to cry, "Why can't anything nice or good happen?" She asked as she turned to cuddle into me. I grabbed hold of the bags in one hand, took her hand in the other and we walked away. I could see the disappointment in her face, I couldn't allow her to lose hope. I told her there were lots of homeless people who needed our help, so let's keep walking until we find someone who needs all this stuff." A smile inched across her face as within two streets, we came across a café for the homeless full of people, young and old, all having an equally hard time for whatever the reason in their lives. We took the bags inside, and they were graciously received by the staff. This good turn made Grace feel better and seeing her happy made me feel even better. Everything about Grace had a domino effect, this time for the better.

We had to take a taxi to the hotel after that, Grace had become extremely tired. The warm room was a welcoming sight. I prepared a bubble bath for her and sat with her while she relaxed soaking away her aches and pains. There was a knock at the door, I opened it to find the waiter with a tray of warm cookies and two large glasses of hot chocolate coated in cream and chocolate shavings. He handed the tray to me saying "Compliments of the hotel". Grace was really pleased, she lay on the bed in her oversized, fluffy dressing gown snacking on cookies and sipping the hot chocolate, telling me how good life is.

I sat by her bedside and watched her fall asleep; she was exhausted yet still smiling while she slept peacefully. I remember looking at her and thinking of what I would do without her unable to see her ever again, it felt unbearable. I explored each curve of her face etching it into my memory saving it forever.

That night we both slept better than we had done for weeks. Grace woke desperately hungry and ate more at breakfast that morning than she had in ages. Later that morning she wanted to visit the Edinburgh dungeons; it was something she had always wanted to do but had never got around to doing it. She howled laughing as I was chosen from the crowd to take part in the show. She thoroughly enjoyed it and as we left she held my arm and said, "That exceeded all my expectations, just as my life has."

We arrived at the station early, in plenty of time to

reserve our place on the platform. We ordered coffee and I stood by her while she took the only available seat in the crowded station. While we were waiting, a song began to play in the background over the tannoy. It was one of her favourite Motown songs and I heard her quietly singing along, totally out of tune. I started to take a video of her, pointing out her singing was terrible. The music became louder and a crowd began to gather around the front of the small café. A man, standing by himself, started singing along to the tune, he had a fabulous voice and the crowed were captivated. Within a few moments, another man randomly joined in, closely followed by a large woman sitting on a bench nearby. Grace jumped up from her seat shouting, "It's a flash mob. Oh my God, Jacob I have always wanted to see one of those." By the time they were at the next chorus, there were over thirty people dancing and singing, awaiting passengers cheered and danced along with the music. Soon there were everyday commuters dancing to the music and holding their phones filming the extraordinary scenes.

Grace's eyes sparkled with excitement as she watched the show, she didn't need to say a word. I could see the music flowing from her soul along with the joy in her eyes. By the end of the song a young girl, who had been watching and cheering with everyone else, screamed with excitement as her boyfriend got down on one knee and proposed. Tears filled Grace's eyes, she tried to wipe them away with her gloved hands. She watched the girl say, "yes, yes, yes." much to the amusement of the watching crowd.

After all the excitement we boarded the train and slumped into our seats and started to plan our time for the following week. We thought we would go to the cinema after work the day before Grace's next chemotherapy treatment.

I noticed a young Asian couple sitting opposite with a small boy of about four and a newborn baby. No one could help but notice these two beautiful children, quite obviously the pride and joy of their parents. The little boy played quietly with a wooden train, pushing it up and down across the table, making soft train noises and pretending to be the controller. He smiled as the conductor came round to check our tickets and watched in amazement as they were scanned. He spoke quietly to his father "I will do that when I am big too, papa," he said as the conductor walked away. His parents however were distracted, trying to calm the cries of their new baby, they kept apologising to us for the disturbance. "It's fine we're not bothered by the noise at all," Grace said reassuringly. "Do you have children?" the lady asked Grace. I tried to think of discreet response but was interrupted by a confident Grace who said, "Charlie was our little boy. I can't imagine it's easy, it must be the lack of sleep that is the hardest to cope with?"

The lady smiled and nodded, I held my breath expecting an uncomfortable emotional outburst in the knowledge I wouldn't be able to find the right thing to say but Grace was fine and seemed happy to be able to be able to even mention Charlie. Her confidence in talking about him was uplifting. During the journey home we discussed how bad we would have coped if we had been that couple trying to calm their crying baby.

When we arrived home, Grace fell asleep with her head resting on my shoulder. She slept for over half hour then woke up randomly asking, "Can we go to church tomorrow?" I knew the reason why, it was Charlie's due date or would have been, had things not turned out the way they had. I have never been a religious person but I completely understood why Grace wanted to mark the occasion. I told her I thought it was a good idea and we could go St Matthews, a small quaint little church about two miles from where we lived. It was not something I would ever think of doing myself but Grace insisted it was what she wanted.

The following day we walked down to the church, it was a peaceful, warm summers day. The sun was shining through the stained-glass windows reflecting the colours around the alter. An elderly lady was attentively arranging flowers and she turned and smiled as we walked inside. Grace had never spoken about religion playing a role in her life but she appeared to find some comfort from being in the chapel, religion was something not lost on her. We walked over to the side of the church and lit a candle. I had no idea who we were lighting a candle for but moaned about the fact she made me put money in the collection box. "There is always someone to light a candle for and if we can't think of anyone in particular then we are truly blessed, so there is always a reason to light one, be thankful." "It's a con to relieve you of your money. That sweet old lady over there will run up here when we leave and remove it ready for the next sucker," I said, joking.

Grace laughed, how had I managed to become such a miserly old grump? To this day it still makes me smile.

"We can light one for Charlie," Grace said hitting me with the reality of it all. "We can light a hundred if you want to?" I replied, as I lifted a candle from the box. I found myself lighting a candle and thinking of Grace, trying to conjure up some magic strength for her to get her through the next round of her treatment. It was a visit of mixed emotions but we both left the church comforted in the hope of a new day and a holy blessing.

I was curious so I asked Jacob, "Tell me, do you believe in God and heaven?" He seemed to contemplate for a while but returned the question asking, "Why do you?" I had to think long and hard before I replied, the truth was I didn't have an answer. "I honestly don't know" I replied, realising my pathetic answer was not the one he hoped for. "There have been times in my life when I have been convinced there is a God and then there have been others when I have simply been unsure. I know lots of people get a great deal from their faith and for some, life is faith and faith often their life. I envy people their beliefs and I imagine cancer is one hell of a challenge to anyone's faith but also one of the greatest comforts. Chemotherapy is like the epitome of hell and I struggle to understand how any God could inflict that on people."

"Well Charlotte, I read every single leaflet on chemotherapy and what to expect at each stage of treatment. It was like a tale of doom. It certainly made me question if chemo was an option worth taking, despite being Grace's one and only glimmer of hope. Chemotherapy often didn't go too well and often it was my mother who spent a great deal of time at the hospital sitting and waiting with Grace. I couldn't always be with her. For example, normally a chemo session would have been scheduled for an hour-long treatment but frequently turned into five or six long hours. I couldn't be there all the time for Grace and she was often following her treatment, so sick but I had taken too much time off work and now had to use my time wisely. We couldn't afford for me to be out of work now that Grace was no longer able to work and I was really grateful to my parents for their support. My mother would devote all her time to Grace whenever she needed her and my father became a taxi service, ferrying them to and from hospital appointments.

One particular week there were three scheduled sessions of chemotherapy which turned into one. Grace's veins were no longer capable of taking the strain of the treatment, so a central line had to be fitted into her chest. The 'cold cap' she had opted to wear in order to try and prevent her hair falling out, became an obstacle, causing her constant headaches. Feeling ill had overtaken everything but losing her hair was no longer her priority.

I arrived home from work one day, to find my mother pottering around the kitchen preparing an abundance of food that would feed a small army. She fussed over Grace, who was by now dozing on the sofa tucked up like a baby. I put my keys on the table causing a clatter of noise, much to my mother's disgust so she greeted me with a quiet "Shush" holding her finger to her lips. "She has just gone to sleep, the poor girl is exhausted," she said. Mum continued to give me a run down of how the food was cooked and the washing was clean and folded. She had put clean linen on the bed for when Grace was ready for bed. "I always sleep better on fresh sheets. It's a woman thing, you wouldn't understand, never mind. She can have a shallow bath as long as the line in her chest is kept dry. It does have a shower proof dressing, so not to worry if it gets splashed. I have had your father pick up some baby bath wash so she can have bubbles in her bath and it won't aggravate anything the nurse said. Anyway, your father is outside so I'm off home but make sure you ring me if you need anything at all. Do you hear me, Jacob?" she said, knowing I had not heard a word she had said. "Yes, mother the bath, the food and the sheets," I answered flippantly. She scowled at me and reminded me things were serious, as she left carrying yet another bag of our washing that we were now incapable of doing.

I sat on the armchair and watched Grace sleeping I felt my eyes fill with tears as I watched an extremely vulnerable, weak and pale Grace rest. Everything was starting to slip away from us slowly but surely. My parents' help was invaluable to both of us. My, once strong, vivacious Grace had now become weak and exhausted, reserving her moments of energy for the most important tasks. I poured a glass of whiskey, dismissing the coffee my mother had made. I held my glass high in the air saying out loud, "Cheers cancer you are an absolute bastard."

# Chapter 8

Grace slept for a few hours and awoke feeling groggy and sore. She was determined to return to the church, so she drank her coffee, changed her clothes and within half hour was ready to leave. It was a particularly chilly evening, the wind was howling, blowing against us as we walked up the path. "It's so very beautiful," Grace said, as we walked through the wooden doors. As always, she was right, the light inside the church seemed to warm the light of the stained-glass windows, it almost looked welcoming. There were more people inside than on our first visit. A large group of young girls had just started choir practice. They unpacked their hymn sheets and were chatting away as they removed their coats and took their places along the pews. We walked over to the candle stand where there were three rows of candles, all of which were at different stages of burning and placed our donation into the box without any sarcastic comments from me. I felt humbled the church was there for us that night it was our sanctuary. Being there made us feel close to Charlie, wherever he may be.

Grace took two candles and handed one to me. She lit hers and placed it carefully on the stand. I lit mine, using the wick of another, which had almost burned out. I suddenly thought I wonder who lit that candle, were they as broken hearted as us? You know Charlotte, people don't talk about grief because it's depressing, and sad. I imagine the individual who lit the candle before me must have gone about their daily routine without anyone appreciating how much of a loss they felt deep inside. Grace must have read my mind as she too commented on the number of candles burning away and how much grief they must represent in this world. "Do you think people ever really get over losing someone or do they just learn to live without them?" Grace asked.

"I've no idea but as life is for us at the minute, I think it's the latter, as people do whatever they have to in order to get by." Grace smiled and held my hand and as we went to leave, the choir started to sing. For the first time in my life, I felt as if I was listening to a 'chorus of angels.' I saw Grace's teary eyes, as she placed her hat on her head. There was a lump in my throat, I thought if I started crying that night I might never have stopped. We held hands as we walked home, talking about what Charlie might be doing if he were still here with us. She smiled as she described how babies change so quickly and how she thought by now he would probably look more like me.

She asked me if I ever thought about him? I wanted to be honest and say most of my time was taken up thinking about her but that was not what she wanted to hear, so I lied and said yes. I didn't need to ask her if she thought about him because I knew he never left her mind however I was certainly not prepared for what she was about to say to me.

"When the doctor told me there was no cure for my cancer, a small part of me felt relieved because when my time comes and I die, I'll be with Charlie. I even thought maybe this cancer is for that reason so I can be with him. Perhaps I need to be there for him and take care of him, wherever that may be. In a way it took the overwhelming feeling of grief away because I know I will be with him one day soon." I felt myself start to get angry and told her to stop talking like that. I even said the immortal selfish words, "and what about me?" "I won't leave you Jacob, none of us are getting off this planet alive, it's just I am going earlier than expected that's all. I'll be waiting for you, we both will. You will have so much to tell us about your future life here and we will be waiting to hear all about it." She spoke with such conviction she almost convinced me she was right and I had no reason to be upset. She always had a way of seeing things, in ways, which never even crossed my mind.

On the Friday of that week, she was so exhausted. Her hair had become brittle, her body was becoming painfully thin and fragile. I drove her to the hospital for her next chemotherapy and the walk from the car to the ward was too much for her, she had to stop and sit down to rest twice along the way in order to gather her strength. The nurse came in to take her bloods as usual but within the hour we were told her bloods were out of range and the chemotherapy couldn't go ahead. The doctor came to talk to us and said it would be better to go home and rest for a few days, they would review her blood count after her body had a little more time to recover. They arranged for the district nurse to visit at home to take care of the line in her chest and to see if we needed anything.

That evening Grace went straight to bed. I sat on my own in a well of self-pity as I looked through old photographs of happier times. She never stirred as I climbed into bed that night, she seemed beyond exhausted. The next morning, she shuffled from the shower to the living room like an eighty-year-old woman. She kept the towel tied around her head as if to prevent her fragile hair from falling out. Twice the towel fell off and she was so upset as handfuls of hair lingered within the towel. "Well, it's happening," she said as she sifted out the long tufts of hair through her fingers and not for the first time, I had no idea what to say, so I said nothing.

There was suddenly a very well-timed knock at the door, which saved me from trying to think of a suitable response. I opened the door to a nurse in a navy-blue uniform with white piping trim around the collar of the dress, obscured by a smart blue outdoor coat. She introduced herself as Naïve the district nursing sister from the local doctor's practice. She spoke with a gentle Irish accent with friendly blue eyes. Her hair was pinned up in a tidy twist held by numerous hairgrips. She came in and took off her coat as she introduced herself to Grace. I offered her a cup of tea, and she sat down next to Grace on the edge of the sofa. She took a pack from her large bag and went to the bathroom to wash her hands. Grace started to panic telling me to follow her and take her clean towels; embarrassed our bathroom might be untidy. Grace shouted out her apologies. I remember thinking these things should not matter at a time like this but they obviously mattered to her. Naïve said it was fine and any towel would do. She said some houses she visited she needed to take her own tissues because the towels looked like doormats, which made Grace laugh. She opened her pack and cleaned and redressed the central line inserted in her chest.

She explained she had dressed it with an extra waterproof dressing so Grace could enjoy a bath without having to worry. Grace appeared more relaxed in her presence, she seemed confident in what Naïve had to say, asking her numerous questions, which had never crossed my mind. She said for at least the next few days Grace was to rest as much as possible and to contact the nurses if she was concerned about anything at all. She left a prescription, for me to collect from the chemist and store in a safe place. The prescription was for a range of injections which Grace might need for sickness or pain if she became unable to tolerate or manage her oral medication.

Her visit seemed to give Grace a bit of a boost because over the next week or so she picked up, becoming more active and much less tired. We went out for short walks and even managed at trip to the local pub on the waterfront, where she drank a small fruity gin as we watched the ships sail by. During that week we met two more nurses, Fatima and Emma and Grace was always pleased to see them both. They always knew the right thing to say and at the right time. She felt confident with their advice and that was the most important thing for her wellbeing.

Grace arranged for the nurses to visit often when I wouldn't be at home and I assumed there were things she wanted to discuss which she might have felt uneasy about with me around. My sister, Lucy, would often call round with the children, and I know Grace loved seeing them. They seemed to be spending more time together talking about the children and what they had been up to that day, it provided Grace with a certain sense of normality. I was delighted when I received a call from my sister telling me they had arranged some special event and that Grace was really excited However the joy was short lived as their plan began to fold. I kind of guessed what it was before she told me and my heart sank.

"You are getting married," Lucy said excitedly. She went on to tell me about all the plans they had made together. The timing, the venue, the flowers, and the photographer, our very own small, intimate celebration. Things had been looking so positive; the ultimate consequence of the diagnosis had been pushed to the back of my mind where I didn't have to deal with it. Now it was back because I knew the reason behind the wedding and the rush to get things arranged was due to the limited time left for us to be together. We were to be married a week later in the local chapel. Lucy was on a mission arranging everything. She organised a special marriage licence with the help of Grace's consultant. Once cleared the arrangements went into hyper drive."

At that very moment on that cold windy roof, I chuckled, recalling my dreams of me being that beautiful bride, walking down the aisle. "You know what Jacob, my hopes of being married; making that commitment to someone who you actually want to spend the rest of your life with, was all I ever wanted. I always thought Nigel was the one I wanted but now after the deceit, the rejection and the web of lies, I am more than happy to never meet anyone, ever again."

Jacob agreed with my sentiment saying, "I never allow myself to dream about the excitement of planning my wedding because that dream very quickly became my worst nightmare.

"Grace spent the full week enthusiastically making plans, as brides do. The small celebration became larger by the day, with extra people added to the guest list. My mother clucked around like a mother hen ordering cake. She shopping for a hat that wasn't too large otherwise that would ruin the day. It had to be exactly the right shade with the right feather to match her handbag. The fuss that comes with weddings allowed people to forget the reasons behind the immediate rush to get this done, for a little while it became a welcome distraction. Everyone discussed their outfits and colours schemes, the house became a hive of industry. Pictures of various styles of bridesmaid dresses and material samples were pushed under my nose, in a vain attempt at making me feel I was a party to the decision-making process. I felt like my father, I learned to nod in agreement in all the right places and at all the right times.

After work that week I came home and cooked supper, when the food was almost ready, I went into the bedroom to see what was taking Grace so long. I walked into the room protesting at the fact my expert cooking was going to be ruined only to be quickly silenced when I saw her sleeping on the bed wrapped in her towel, surrounded by a library of bridal magazines. I stopped in my tracks as I watched her while she slept, she looked so happy and contented and peaceful, the perfect bride to be. I covered her in a warm thick blanket and returned to the kitchen.

I sat flicking through my phone looking at the photographs of our holiday trips. As I did so an idea for a special wedding present came to mind. I scoured the internet and found a company which made blankets with printed pictures imposed on them, so I decided to send off a collage of pictures of our life together, including a selection of Grace whilst she was pregnant with Charlie. There was a picture I had taken one morning when she had run into the room swearing Charlie bump had grown overnight. We had taken lots of pictures from a side profile and had drawn smiley faces on the bump. I placed the photo with the smiley face in the middle of the blanket because although I had no doubt of her love for me, Charlie was forever her world.

The day of the wedding arrived so quickly, I was sent to have breakfast with my father while the women collectively clucked around Grace and Lucy's children at our house. They had allocated rooms for different functions, such as hairdressers and nail technicians. The doorbell rang constantly with the deliveries of flowers and gifts arriving. The kitchen that had been cleaned to within an inch of its life, was a hive of activity, as trays after trays of food were prepared and served. The kettle seemed to be permanently on boil and cups topped up. There were numerous compliments of 'that's beautiful' and 'stunning.' There was no sadness, no talk of illness, everyone made sure it remained that way. The photographer followed the ladies around all morning, taking hundreds of pictures capturing every moment.

Feeling completely out of place and with everyone reminding me of the superstition and bad luck on seeing the bride before the wedding, I ended up spending the morning with my father. I let myself into my mother's house to see two immaculately pressed suits hanging in the hallway one for my father and one for me. He was nowhere to be seen as I walked into the lounge, so I went out into the kitchen and noticed the shed door at the end of the garden was slightly open. There was a small plume of smoke rising out above the door. "It's a good place to enjoy my pipe in peace without your mother hanging around, moaning," he said as he blew the smoke, with the distinct smell of tobacco, into the air. Sitting on one of his two deck chairs in his shed he looked relaxed and calm, a complete contrast to our house with all of the chaos. He offered me the pipe as I sat down in the chair next to him, "How long do we have before we have to go to get there on time?" my father asked. "About two hours," I replied. He asked me if I was nervous, as he re-lit his pipe, which by this point had gone out. "Not nervous no, I just find it all a bit overwhelming, particularly with everything else that is going on. I just want her to be happy, dad. She is going through so much I want this to be her big day," I answered.

My father leaned back in his chair and said, "I know you think you are her saviour son, the one who does the manly stuff but you're kidding yourself. The truth is, you put the bins out and you hold her hand when you go out for walks, if there's a noise downstairs in the middle of the night you are the first to go and investigate just incase it's a burglar, so you can fight him off to keep her safe. That's where the stereotypical man of strength ends, because son, from that point the protector role ends. We men are who we are because our women put us there. Don't ever doubt Grace is your strength, son. You are everything you are because of her. We reach up and achieve because we stand on their shoulders. The reason you are so terrified to be without her, is not just the grief, it is because you know you will have to reach for what you want without being able to stand on her shoulders. Don't you dare tell your mother I admitted all this but women are the stronger sex. Give them a house they make you a home, give them a baby, they make you a family, give them your love and they do magic with it. We men are simple creatures; things to us are simply black and white. We fail to see the variety of colours in life, only they have the talent to bring it to us. You have an opportunity today to make her day something really special. It's about you two and the people around you that you love. She will give you memories which you will keep forever son, in fact we will all keep forever." My father's profound and eloquent words opened a waterfall of emotion for me. I cried like a snotty nosed child unable to control myself. "I am so fucked dad; I don't know what I am going to do. I don't know what I am doing from one day to the next, it's all so unfair." I held my head in my hands and cried at the very thought of being without her. My father was not the tactile type and so the pat on the knee I received was the equivalent of his manly hug.

"As far as I remember son, you never came with a written promise that life would be fair. We're all going through this with you and if I could take your heartbreak from you, I would do it in a heartbeat. You'll cope because you have to, that's life. You're just going to have to get on, the way we all have to. Life is fleeting and the older you get the more you realise just how fleeting it really is and how fragile it can be. We all just plod along doing our best, regardless of any hurt or tears son, you are the luckiest man on the planet because to know love as you have, is as rare as hen's teeth. You need to remember that because very few people find true love however long they live. Today though, as your mother keeps reminding me (usually through tears) is not a day for sadness, it's going to be a great day, so come on let's get showered, suited and booted or I will have to do time for the pipe smoke."

We left for the wedding, driving in my car, saying very little on the journey. As we pulled around the corner of the church gates I could see friends and family dressed in their Sunday best, waiting around outside. I started to become nervous faced with the enormity of the event. My father climbed out of the car and stood next to the driver's side door. "Are you ready son?" he repeated his words, lost on me in my daze.

"Ready as I will ever be," I replied, as we walked towards the entrance of the church. The concept of no sorrow had already gone straight out of the window, as my aunt Janice immediately burst into tears as soon as she greeted us. The vicar walked across to welcome us but was rudely pushed to one side by my aunt trying to hold back her tears, clutching at her handkerchief. At the same time, she attempted to adjust my tie which had been perfectly knotted before she interfered. The vicar escorted us to one side and talked through the proceedings, where we should stand and where we should walk. He walked with us to the front of the church and pointed out our seats.

The best man was my lifelong school friend, Ollie; I had known him since primary school, we had grown up together and I can't remember any stage in my life when he was not around. He was my rock these days, more so lately as he kept me going, supporting me through each and every day. We sat together in the front pew saying very little, looking like a pair of nervous schoolboys waiting outside the headmaster's office. Ollie kept checking his pocket for the ring, each time breathing a sigh of relief as he reassured himself it was still there. He jokingly said he hoped his girlfriend, Kate, didn't catch Grace's bouquet, he didn't want her getting any wrong ideas and we both laughed.

A steady procession of guests started to filter into the church, it was nearly time for the ceremony to begin, then right on cue the organ music started to play, I could feel the tension grow. The vicar nodded in our direction and we both stood up. First in the procession were my nieces who scattered petals along the aisle from little straw baskets. Sounds of, "awwweee" from the guests were heard, as they continued to walk down the aisle in their beautiful dresses and flowered headbands, followed by Grace, so rightfully owning the limelight. I know the bridegroom always sees their bride walk down the aisle and is often utterly overwhelmed, I often thought it was somewhat of an exaggeration. I have never underestimated something so much in all my life; I was immediately floored with emotion, I have never seen any woman look so beautiful; it was hard to believe she was actually walking towards me and wanted to marry me, of all people.

Her hair was pinned up with flowers, she looked so healthy and vibrant. Her cheeks glowed and her eyes sparkled. She held onto my father's arm, as he beamed with pride to be the one to give her away. She had a blue, silk ribbon hanging from her flowers which held a tiny photograph of Charlie; it was her way of including him into our special day. I remembered that photograph, bringing back his memory to me. Grace of course, didn't need any reminder; he never left her thoughts for a second. I honestly cannot tell you what style her wedding dress was, not because I didn't care but because all I could see was her. To this day her smile at that very moment is engraved in my memory.

Our vows were written by my sister, Lucy, she said they reflected our individual personalities and anyway no one wanted to hear Grace say the words, 'till death us do part.' Grace smiled from ear to ear throughout the swearing of our vows, unable to contain her happiness. Some members of the congregation were in tears as we walked down the aisle as man and wife. Grace said loudly to the tearful congregation, "it's time to party."

With the car decked out with trailing cans and covered in ribbons and banners, we made a detour to place Grace's bouquet on Rose's headstone, Grace said she would have so loved her to have been there. The sadness of the day started and ended there at the graveside and that evening everything went without a hiccup.

We celebrated into the small hours, Grace rarely leaving the dance floor. Our wedding guests had clubbed together and paid for us to stay at a very posh hotel not too far from home, so we both soon collapsed into our hotel bed in sheer exhaustion. The following morning, we had cooked breakfast served in our room and the had the luxury of lounging around in our dressing gown's the following day, which was just what the doctor ordered. We spent the next couple of days enjoying the more sophisticated things in life, such as taking a swim before breakfast. We wandered around the grounds and took our time deciding when to have lunch. We were allocated our own private table and personal waiter in the Huntsman's lounge, courtesy of the hotel. We ate Michelin star food chatting endlessly about everything and nothing of any importance. We looked over pictures of our wedding night and laughed at the memories and then I gave Grace her gift. When she opened the box, she wept as she examined the pictures on the blanket, stroking the picture of her 'Charlie bump'

"What if there is nothing after this life, Jacob?" she asked as she kissed the picture of Charlie on the blanket. "There is, I am sure of it," as if I had inside knowledge of such things. "What if there isn't though? It scares me, I think it's the only part of dying that really scares me," she said. "Listen, if there is nothing then what does it matter because none of us will know will we? The one thing that is a certainty in life is that we are all going to die at some point in time, the only uncertainty is when." I tried to reassure her applying some of her own teachings. She cuddled into me as we lay on the bed, covering both of us with the blanket. "Like the doctors said, you and I don't know how much time we have left together, it could be so much longer than predicted. New cures are discovered all the time, so what we need to do is just concentrate on the here and now and keeping you as well as we possibly can."

Seven weeks passed and Grace seemed to be doing really well, life reverted back to some kind of semblance of normality in the circumstances. She had been given a course of steroids and a break from the chemotherapy which seemed to do her the world of good. Confident in her progress, I returned to work and mum and dad drove her to and from the appointments at the hospital. Grace was booked in for the first of her fourth cycle of chemotherapy for ten one particular Tuesday morning. So, I planned a takeaway and movie night, a relaxing evening as Grace often returned drained and sleepy. I had slipped out of the office at lunchtime to buy some chocolate and wine, when I received a call from my father saying I should go straight home.

I arrived to find my Mother in tears being comforted by my sister. My father met me in the hallway, where he patted me on the shoulder and said, "It's hard son, you have to just do your best." He left trying to hide his bloodshot eyes under orders to walk the dog. Grace was sitting on the sofa next to Naïve. I didn't have to ask what was going on as Grace looked up and said "I can't have any more chemotherapy; it isn't going to kill the cancer and it's making me so very ill. I've spoken to the doctor and we have decided it's time to stop." I gazed at Grace in utter disbelief. Initially my immediate reaction was of anger wanting to know how she could make such a decision without speaking to me. My mother became very upset when I shouted out in temper, begging me to stay calm. Naïve discreetly took my mother and sister to one side and suggested this may be a good time to get some fresh air to give us time to digest the news. I sat with my head in my hands full of rage, as Grace sat totally impassive. I smashed my hands on the table in sheer indignation at Grace's defiant decision, can you believe it Grace didn't utter a word, she just stood up and left the room."

As I sat on the cold roof listening to his frustration and devastation, I could feel the anger in his voice more than his words. It was an impossible decision they were both forced to face. Sometimes when all you have is hopeless hope, who knows if it would be easier to let go and take control or to hang on to it as your final link to life. I could see, even now, no answer would ever give him peace. I wondered if the strength she had found in making her decision somehow made him feel weak at a time when she was being unbelievably brave and resilient. Either way it was an ongoing torture for him to bear.

He continued to tell me how Naïve handed him a coffee, "She calmly told me that while Grace had obviously been a party to the decision in ending the treatment, it was highly unlikely the doctor would have continued with her treatment because her blood readings were so out of range. The risk of treating her with any further chemotherapy could make her worse. I just turned to her in anger and said, "Which part of "if she doesn't get chemo she is dead" do you, so called professionals, not understand?" Naïve appeared unphased by my outburst, she just waited until I calmed down a little and then told me directly and to the point. "Jacob, Grace is dying and there is no treatment which can save her. The cancer has spread to her lungs, liver and spine. The decision to stop will allow her to have some quality time with you while she feels reasonably well enough. It is quality time she needs to put her affairs in order and end her days in a way she can control. She doesn't want her final days or weeks or months to be filled with hospital appointments and feeling so ill after even more chemotherapy. Spending time with you was a major factor in reaching her decision." I laughed out aloud as I repeated the words, 'quality time.' "Is that what you call quality time, sitting next to your wife watching her as the cancer kills her? Jesus, what do you do for thrills if that's quality?" I just broke down and sobbed, I couldn't speak but Naive was extremely supportive despite my cruel words. I continued sobbing until my head and my heart ached, life is just so unfair.

# Chapter 9

There was a huge, sudden loud bang, as car in the street below backfired followed by a scream, we both rather abruptly found ourselves back in the moment, sitting on the roof of the car park. "Look! up there, a man is going to jump off the roof," I heard a woman's voice scream from down below us. I was so engrossed in Jacob's tragic narrative, the freezing cold wind on the roof and the threat of his suicide had been forgotten. Jacob placed his head in his hands and sighed, "Oh God." Now even more than ever, I didn't know what to say. I suppose I thought while he was talking nothing was going to happen. His life story had taken us both away from the cold roof and the present reality, back into his past and his memories. Jacob's expression changed, he became extremely nervous and very irritated quite quickly. I shuffled forward from the relative comfort of the air-vent, which had provided me limited protection from the wind. I felt like reaching out and grabbing hold of him. My stomach turned at the thought of him shuffling along that thin ledge. I was scared he might fall by accident from sheer nerves. Sirens could be heard in the distance and this time I had no doubt they were for him.

I shuffled myself around the corner to get closer to him "Jacob please don't do anything rash, please I'm begging you." His whole demeanor altered, his whole-body language gave me concern, he was very apprehensive, he looked exasperated but scared. "Anything rash? Are you fucking mad? I'm about to fucking well die. I can't jump or jump because I'm a spineless bastard." He started crying, "I don't even want to die. I just want this life to end. I just don't want to live anymore. Grace didn't have a choice and she was braver than me. I have a choice and I can't even get that right." "You do have a choice though, that is the point. Would this really be what Grace would want from you?" I said, as if I knew what I was talking about. He turned and looked at me, the anger on his face evident, as he responded, "What does it matter what she might want, she has been dead for three years, she is just ashes." Tears ran down his face; tears of devastation, as he spoke through teeth gripped with crushing emotion. "You are not pathetic; this is all so overwhelming, no one knows what to do. That's why it's not the norm and people are shouting and sirens are sounding. This is an emergency; we are talking about the rest of your life right now."

"Charlotte will you please go away and leave me alone. I have been sitting here with you for hours, telling you I have no life, so ending it is the next step. I'm that man who never got over the grief of losing his wife, people will understand. I'm that depressive bloke that pretends everything is all right, when all the while I feel like I am trapped inside my own head, everyday a constant battle to try and stop killing myself. My mother sees it in my eyes, I know she does because mothers who love, see everything. She lives with the torture everyday that she might bury her son. My father walks around saying shit like… 'man up' in the hope that I will think, oh yeah 'good idea' I never thought of that.

"I don't imagine your father means to be so condescending, it's just something people say and his way of coping," Jacob seemed to agree, although he spoke through angry tears. "My father is literally the father we all hope to be one day. There is nothing exciting about him, as children we nicknamed him 'Dangerous Dave' because he was so boring. He never talks about himself or his own life; he talks about mum and us. He is my hero really, which makes this situation so much worse. Measuring up against him I am a total and utter failure in life I couldn't even look after my own wife and son. If I could have been half the father he is, life would have been amazing but that wasn't meant to be, was it? Literally my life is one enormous mess, fundamentally floored and impossible to put right. The thought of suicide sits on my shoulders every day like some devil's voice whispering in my ear and it becomes all so time consuming."

"You're still here, so there must be some part of you that wants to live?" I said in the hope he will think of something which may tip the balance of his thoughts. "I'm still here because I'm pathetic and haven't been able to end it all, that's it," he sounded deflated in his answer, as if he had just come to terms with the fact.

"I know all about being pathetic. I am the master of pathetic, you don't even come close," I said with great conviction. Jacob didn't look up, he just held his head as if what I had said was too stupid to acknowledge. "I'm so pathetic, I told my best friend how I found underwear in my boyfriend's bag and assumed they were a present for me. I put them on as a surprise, ready for him coming home. Even when he said he had a sudden massive headache and wasn't up to it, I still didn't realise the underwear wasn't meant for me and him seeing me parading around almost naked was enough to turn his stomach." Jacob said nothing and just looked over at me. The fire brigade had arrived and cordoned off an area below, underneath where he was sitting balanced on the ledge. A policewoman suddenly appeared in the doorway of the stairwell, obviously assessing the situation. Without turning around, Jacob told me to tell them to go away otherwise he would jump. I shouted over to the officer but wasn't too sure whether my words were lost, carried away in the wind.

"You're not pathetic Charlotte, it's his loss. He's done you a favour, it's just hard for you to see at the moment," Jacob said. His praise almost made me cry, here he was in the depths of despair and he was trying to make me feel better about my own life.

"I understand the uselessness and stupidity feeling Jacob. I've been called stupid for so long now, true or not, it has become who I am. You know I once, unexpectedly bumped into Nigel, my ex, he was going into a cookie shop while I was out shopping. I walked up behind him, thinking it would be a nice surprise. He wasn't surprised at all, he just said I had startled him. The lady at the counter handed him a cookie box, which I excitedly intercepted and opened thinking they were for me. I thanked him for being so thoughtful, only to find a picture of a baby on the cookie. He quickly snatched it away from me and handed it back to the perplexed lady behind the counter saying she had given him the wrong cookie box. I believed him without a single shred of doubt in my mind. Even as we left the shop and I asked why he was not at his Judo class, he snapped at me for being too intrusive, I even apologised! I am stupid and gullible and a hopeless romantic, destined to have my heart trodden on. Even a week later when I saw a similar cookie box at my best friend's house while chatting over coffee and I started telling her the funny story, not for one second did it enter my thick brain the baby cookie box was actually for her and he was a total cheat and liar and that she was a part of those lies."

I understand guilt, Jacob I honestly do. After I found out they were having this affair and a baby, I hounded them both for months. I behaved like I was possessed. I would sit outside their house in the car watching them have a life. I don't even know what good I expected to come from it, it was just an instinctive desire. It became like a bizarre form of self-torture, hoping to see them arguing or their life being generally shit but I didn't, I saw them having a normal life, it was like being stabbed in the back on an hourly basis. I was stalking them so often; it became my normality; I even started to take a pack lunch with me because I was spending too much money buying snacks. I would scrutinise their social media at least twice a day, reading every comment and photograph. The typical Christmas poses in the matching pyjamas, saying "mummy to be" with an arrow pointing to the word 'bump' which practically sent me over the edge.

You know one day as I sat in the car, I had stomach pains that were so bad, I had to go home via the chemist who asked me if the tablets were for me and was I pregnant. My life had been so wrapped up with Nigel it had not even crossed my mind I had not had a period for over three months. I bought a testing kit and rushed home. It was a huge adrenaline rush to see the test come out as positive, not because I wanted a baby but as a final act of power over Nigel. It was something I could use to ruin their smug, oh so happy life and carry out my ultimate revenge. Would you believe it? I planned my ambush, not really giving any thought to the baby. I grinned as I perfected a plan to go to their baby shower and announce my news.

A few days later I suddenly started getting abdominal pains. They became really bad and quickly, I had to climb out of the bath and telephone for an ambulance. I sat on the floor of the bathroom unable to move in pain, which became intolerable, then I could see the baby in its tiny form lying in the pool of blood on my bathroom floor. I could clearly see the shape of the head and a small body. I picked it up and wrapped it in tissue.

That evening I cried myself to sleep. I was wracked with the guilt that I had not cared for my tiny baby. I had lost the baby because I only saw them as my tool for revenge. Bad, brings bad and that's exactly what I had been, bad with revenge taking over my life. I decided to take my little baby to my father's grave and place them under a rose bush on the grave, asking him to take care of it for me. Perhaps I was, in some small way, trying to ease my guilt.

In a bizarre twist of fate, the loss of my baby diverted me away from my revenge, getting my own back didn't seem important anymore. I was determined now, more than ever to get on with my life and stop living in a state of continuous heartbreak, and I know I will never forget what happened, the guilt will stay with me forever. Don't you see Jacob, if you jump that will stay with me too. Suicide really doesn't stop the pain; all it does is compound your pain and passes it on to the next person in a more concentrated form of torture.

That tiny new life made me deal with my anger and face my realities and shortcomings. Oh, I was devastated that Nigel didn't love me, he never could because he loved her. I was furious, she happened to be my best friend; we had been through so much together over the years. She was there through school and the death of my father. We shared our teens and all the experiences and dreams that went alongside that. Most of all, I was angry with myself for not realising it was going on right under my very nose. Anger has to be dispensed with, otherwise it turns into a vitriolic behaviour and then inevitably becomes integral to your life. I had to deal with my anger and move on, losing the baby made me realise what I was doing, I see that now. I honestly worry that karma might keep making me pay for my inhumanity and jealousy, ensuring I am single forever and of course never have children."

"Exactly like me then?" Jacob answered. "Yes, I think it looks like we are in the same boat. However, unlike you, I refuse to hand down my shitty baton for someone else to deal with," I answered. Jacob became agitated saying, "how dare you judge me, you know nothing about the reasons behind the decisions I have made in my life, they are nothing at all like yours, you know nothing about me at all."

"Well, that is a fine high horse," I said sarcastically. "But I do know your mother and father will slowly die inside if you jump. I know if you do jump it will change my life forever. You say being selfish is your biggest regret, well what you are doing now is the most selfish thing you can ever do to those close to you, it will hurt them forever." I retorted in anger.

Jacob looked back to face me and said, "I wish you would just fuck off and go away. I don't want to hear your sob stories or the lecturing. Take your philosophies on life and get out of my mine, leave me to fuck up my own life as I choose. It's none of your business." He turned his back on me to dismiss any response I might have forthcoming, and so for the next few minutes we both sat in complete silence.

Then out of the blue Jacob broke the awkward silence "Did they have their baby, Nigel and your friend?" "Yes, they had a little girl, they named her Sophie. I think they're happy and I'm pleased for both of them but I don't really think about them anymore. To be honest I think more about my own baby and I wonder how life might have been if things had been different," "Well aren't you the sanctimonious picture of forgiveness," he responded sarcastically. In my defence I replied, "I'm just saying your anger is why you are here and going through all this." Jacob threw his hands into the air "My god you are a genius! I fucking well know I'm angry, in fact I'm bastard well furious. I have done the entire deep breathing thing, the practicing of forgiveness, it's all bullshit. I'm angry and I want to be. This is who I am and I don't want to feel good about the death of my wife."

The wind started to gust, once again it felt so cold and I could see Jacob shivering. "I have a heat pad in my bag if you would like it," and I started rummaging through my bag. "It would need to be the size of a sheet to warm me up, I think," he answered, as I returned the five-inch, square heat pad back into my bag, realising its inadequacy in the circumstances. I tried to make light of the situation by saying, "you could place it on your chest, resting it against your heart it might thaw out a little." Jacob laughed, "you could be right and I might even learn to forgive a little."

"I feel a little better since I have forgiven Nigel and my best friend, it's really quite therapeutic. I think, probably, the worst part was losing my best friend and not seeing it coming. As friends go, she was the best. We were so close for such a long time. She looked out for me like a wing man. When everything came out about my father and his secret life, I was a laughingstock at school. Kids can be so cruel and they would tease me, "I'm your sister or am I your brother' as they taunted me in the playground. She stuck by me, constantly telling me to ignore them; she was there for me when it mattered.

"Why on earth would it ever cross your mind she would deceive you in such away, cheating with your man, and she was your best friend? If we all went around thinking the worst and never trusting anyone no matter what, life would be intolerable," Jacob said, as if the counseling roles had now been reversed and it was me who needed guidance. "I amaze myself at my own level of gullibility Jacob, I am the epitome of that 'stupid woman.' I believe anything, that suits me at the time, rather than face the ugly truth. I honestly live in a dream world and then I wonder why I am let down so easily.

I remember Nigel received an award at work and I was so proud to be with him. He was so intelligent; he worked in engineering really excelling in his field of expertise. I spent weeks planning my outfit, I wanted to look glamorous, booking appointments for my hair, tan, nails, the full works. It was a really classy, black-tie event and as a special surprise I bought him an expensive watch, one I knew he had always coveted. I'm not joking when I say it cost me thousands. I arrived home early that evening to surprise him, I tiptoed in through the front door quietly, to leave it for him to find on the table and planned to hide to watch his reaction. I could hear him talking in the bedroom, pleased he was distracted, I crept into the front room and placed the watch wrapped up with a bow, on the table, beside his car keys. I didn't give a second thought as to what or with whom he was having his conversation, I just hid in the hallway. I could hardly control my excitement as I caught a glimpse of him, dressed smartly in his tuxedo, walking around in the bedroom.

As I watched, I heard his phone ring and heard someone say, "Sorry I'm on my own now, let me see what you look like?" I realised he was using his iPad and was on face time. I tried to hear who the other person was but in my clumsy effort to hide, as I moved closer, I knocked the flowers off the side table, causing a loud crash. Nigel came running out thinking we were being burgled, to find me pulling wet flowers from my tights and apologising profusely.

He was angry and asked what the hell I was doing hiding and despite my best efforts to explain, he became even more morose. When I asked who he was talking to, he reminded me of the fact I was not a detective, he was a grown man who didn't have to explain himself to me or indeed anyone?

Despite all my best efforts the evening was a shambles, his bad mood continued throughout the entire evening, it seemed like something and nothing at the time. However later on that week I met some friends for a drink and a catch up and one of them spoke about her experiences of how men behave towards those they love most.

"You can always tell when men are in love because they want to show off to the one person they want to impress." She went on to prove her point. "I had a friend who went on a dream holiday, cruising around the Mediterranean with her new boyfriend. They went on a tour around the ship and throughout the whole tour the boyfriend was talking to his ex-girlfriend on Skype, showing her how amazing the ship looked on his phone as they continued their tour. When my friend confronted him, he denied that it meant anything but obviously it did because two months later they were back together."

Everyone agreed with her, "They always want to show the good things in life to the one they truly love and want to be with, so he obviously didn't want to be there with her," Steph said, looking very confident in her ruthless answer. "That's rubbish Steph, you do talk shit sometimes," I said, half hoping she was wrong but knowing she wasn't. "I am telling you it is true, my Robbie used to face time me when he was dressed in his suit because he knows how I love a man in a suit. Men like to show off, they are creatures that love to be praised," Steph said as she flicked through her phone to show us a picture of Robbie in a suit, which no one was interested in. It flashed through my mind there and then Nigel was doing exactly that when I walked in that day standing around in his tux. He was displaying his dressed up look for the woman he really loved, like a peacock with its fanned feathers. How long could I carry on kidding myself by making such stupid excuses?

I looked over at Jacob he was looking pale and cold. I

couldn't see the doorway as clearly as before because I had shifted places along the ledge. I could see three police officers waiting in the doorway, obviously planning their next move, trying to buy some time in order to assess the situation. "What do you do, Jacob?" I asked. "Apart from commit suicide you mean, I'm in computers," he answered. "Are you any good?" I asked. "Better than I am at this, yes. Actually sorry, I'm very good and at the top of my game, as people say," almost matter of fact. "What do you do outside work, for a hobby?" by now I probably sounded quite intrusive.

"What's with all of the questions? Are you planning on writing my epitaph? I don't do a lot, I used to be into boats, sailing boats. My father was a professional yachtsman, and when he initially retired, he became a sailing instructor. People used to travel across the country to take lessons from him. We were all brought up surrounded by sailing boats, it was a huge part of our lives as children, even the dog used to come along. Life was good, we spent most of our summers on the lake; it was like a second home. I had planned one day, to spend time on the lake with my own children but it wasn't gonna happen, was it?" He sighed. "Your life isn't over if you don't want it to be. You could still go on and have a good life," I said, hoping he would fine some truth in my answer.

"The police are still there Jacob, there are three of

them. You know they won't leave, don't you? regardless of what I say to them." A police officer's voice shouted over a loud hailer, asking if I was injured, to which I replied, "yes" but my voice was lost in the rattle of the strong winds encircling the roof.

It was weird, I felt I wanted them to leave us alone, as if in some way, this was our time alone on the roof, just ours and they were somehow intruding. I had to keep reminding myself this situation was not one of personal space but of a desperate act of a man I didn't even know.

# Chapter 10

Jacob seemed unruffled by the commotion he had caused, he appeared distracted and disconnected from what was going on around him. The sun had disappeared through the heavy, dense clouds and the daylight seemed to disappear as the sky became even more overcast. The chill in the wind was cutting; my feet and hands were numb with the cold. I removed the contents from inside my handbag, to use as a cushion on the freezing cold floor. Every move I made to make myself slightly warmer or more comfortable, it made me think of how much worse it was for Jacob balancing on that ledge.

Jacob asked if I was okay. I told him I was just a little cold and he quickly pointed out people would be worried about me by now, not knowing where I was. I reminded him that applied to him too and tried to reassure him there were people who cared for him. I thought, perhaps, reminding him of his family he may give them some consideration before making the final decision to jump, ruining their lives in the process.

The look on his face changed immediately, I could see the sadness in his eyes turning to anger. "I bet you're sitting there thinking you can make me see sense by reminding me of all the people I have to live for so I might change my mind? Well for your information the saddest thing about taking your own life is knowing what you are going to do to those you love and still be incapable of preventing it from happening. Everyone says 'if only' they had talked to me and why didn't they talk to me, why didn't they say something? How the hell do you tell someone you love; you want to kill yourself? It's like living with a dark secret, no one could ever possibly understand. Nothing about taking your own life is easy, that's why most people have a good drink, it goes someway to numbing the pain but just enough to achieve the outcome. I am tired of the pain, Charlotte; I am so tired of life. Nothing good feels good anymore and the future is a futile and an incredible effort. You must have seen those Japanese television programs where they run round an impossible assault course no one can ever complete, it's a pure waste of time and effort?" "Yes," I answered, wondering what on earth he was going to say and how it related to why we were here on a roof.

"Well, that's what each day in my life feels like. I feel selfish about the way I am feeling but most of all, I feel totally and utterly humiliated and weak. Weak for allowing myself to feel so empty, while I watched the love of my life battle to spend one more day on this planet. I have no more excuses than the next man but knowing that only makes me feel worse. The idea of death scares the shit out of me but the idea of living makes me want to die. There's no sense in any of it, I'm at a loss, trying to find any sense in it. There are people out there that spend their lives tortured by grief for those they love, wishing they could have saved them, when the truth and the reality is, if they had wanted to be saved, they would have been. They must have carried out that final act knowing at the moment they could not be saved."

Jacob continued "There was this guy, Nick, the husband of a close friend of mine, who took his own life early last year. No one had any idea he was even depressed. One that fateful day he rang his manager at work, it was teatime and he asked if she would mind covering for him as he needed to sort out some family issues. She was slightly surprised but sympathetically agreed. He ended the call saying, "see you soon!" He went home, cooked his children's supper, just as he did every other day, then he went outside to the garage and took his life. His wife found him hanging in their garage.

His family and friends reacted in total and utter shock, they couldn't understand what made him d o such a thing. I remember people saying how he had everything to live for, a beautiful family, a fabulous job, which he loved. However, all these things just make you feel worse about the decision, such an act of desperation. Part of me was actually jealous he had been successful, as if in some way he taken the idea away from me. I can be with Grace and Charlie and all of this pain would disappear. Nick didn't want to be saved in the same way I don't want to be saved. His wife kept on saying if he had only been able to talk to us, he would have seen the light at the end of the tunnel. We would have worked things out.

There are, in fact, two tunnels, people see the good in their life but suicide takes you to in a completely different direction where there is no light or common sense, it just does not exist. It's an irresistible place that keeps pulling you towards it, like a magnet. It's constantly on my mind and it's a struggle to prevent myself actually carrying it out, rather than the decision itself. It has become an obsession, a dark secret no one knows about. Did you know there are even suicide web site chat rooms, where people talk about what is the best way to kill yourself, they even give you tips on what to write if you decide you are leaving a note, making it almost normal so matter of fact!"

"Do you really want to die?" I asked, trying to understand why anyone would really want to do it. I always thought people who committed suicide deep down hoped to be saved the act of suicide I thought it was a cry for help which had gone tragically wrong. "I tried to take my life not long after Grace died. I drank a bottle of whisky and took some paracetamol; I passed out on the couch and was devastated when I was still alive the following morning. A friend found me, having called at the house when I failed to turn up for work. I cried because I failed, she cried at the fact I had tried to kill myself. I apologised and said all the right things, well no one wants to hear you want to die. I had been drinking heavily at the time, so I blamed the alcohol for my decision and promised to get some help. After that she decided to check in on me every day for months. She sent me pictures of people suffering with liver failure as a result of failed overdoses and videos of those who had once thought of suicide and had now turned their lives around. I pretended to be inspired and grateful for all she was doing but truthfully, I always wished I had just taken more tablets and stayed asleep.

I know it's instinctive for people to care; it's what we do naturally. One often hears stories about good things people have done and how they have saved others. Believe it or not, I have learned people can be saved in a variety of ways. I was offered counseling when Grace was ill but I really didn't want anyone to help me feel better, Grace was dying, I wanted it to be painful because that's how it should be. I wanted it to feel it was all too much to cope with because that's how it is. I thought Grace would be ill for a lot longer than she actually was, I really thought we had more time together. I felt betrayed. In reality the doctor never actually gave us a precise time frame, it was, I suppose, an assumption on my part, or maybe it was hope. I didn't even recognise the signs when things were obviously getting so much worse for her, I think I just closed my eyes to it all and pretended everything was going to be okay.

I remember we had invited my friend Ollie and his wife, Kate one evening for a curry. It seemed an opportune time, Grace had been weak but stable for a few weeks. We decided to order a takeaway to make the evening less of a hassle. After a friendly debate about whether it was Chinese or Indian, we agreed to have an Indian and ordered what seemed enough to feed a small army. Grace was quiet during the evening, she didn't say much and a little later said she was feeling unwell, jokingly she said she had eaten too much. I pointed out she only had enough to fill a small tea plate, however she was adamant.

"If you would all excuse me," Grace had said as I saw her walk across into the downstairs bathroom. I noticed, as she was walking, her legs appeared heavy, and I remembered the district nurses has told us about oedema. The skin retains the water that builds up and often causes excessive weight in the legs, making walking difficult. I looked up as she walked towards the door and was horrified to see two large wet patches on the back of Graces trousers. I made an excuse and followed her to the bathroom, just as she closed the door.

I knocked and asked if she was okay, she took a while to answer but said yes. Ollie and Kate were sitting looking uncomfortable, I offered them another drink which they declined then made their excuses to leave. I completely understood and was grateful for their understanding. They were just putting their coats on while I hunted around for their car keys when there was a clatter from the bathroom, I ran to find Grace had fallen over, the bathroom door had flown open with her fall exposing her in all her indignity. I scrambled to try and help her, as did Kate. Grace was screaming in pain and had obviously hurt herself in the fall. I tried, in my own man handling, useless way, to pull her out from the gap into which she had fallen, while Kate took the more dignified approach of trying to protect Grace's modesty. The small space made the task impossible, the very idea of turning a cupboard under the stairs into a small bathroom was never an idea that made any practical sense.

After about twenty minutes trying various methods of trying to free her, Grace asked me to call the nurses. Ollie and Kate left saying repeatedly, they were more than happy to stay and help. I sat on the floor with Grace, who by now was covered in a blanket, taking paracetamol and drinking tea. She must have been in so much pain but she didn't complain. She made light of the undignified manner of the way in which the evening ended. "I can't feel my legs," Grace said. I didn't know what to say. I felt a massive lump growing in my throat as I tried, in vain, to think of an appropriate response that didn't reveal my desperation. My mouth moved but no words came out. I looked at Grace, she smiled saying it would be okay. It was probably a good thing at the minute, as otherwise she would be in a lot more pain from being jammed between the wall and the toilet. Her eyes were full of tears as she spoke. We both knew she was far from okay.

Within half an hour the district nurses knocked at the door. I was relieved, it was as if the cavalry had arrived. Naïve stood there with her bag in her hand and her rain-soaked coat apologising for not arriving sooner. Fatima also made her apologies for being late, explaining she had been delayed with another patient. I stood and watched in total admiration as they took of their coats and within minutes were chatting to Grace, the whole situation completely under control. I was ordered into the kitchen and told to make myself useful by making cups of tea. Naive went into the front room and made a number of phone calls re-assuring me everything was in hand, although she didn't say things were okay and in the absence of okay, I believe it meant 'we were making the best of now what was a bad situation.'

I overheard Grace asking Naïve if this was the beginning of the end? I choked at the thought of her answer. I had no idea what she could or would say in such circumstances. Naïve continued seeing to Grace, the questioning didn't deter her in the slightest, "Sweetheart, if I had an answer for everyone who asked me that question, I would be reading your future on a sea front and charging you for the pleasure! Grace, only

God, in whatever form you believe in him, knows the answer to that one. So, for now let us get you off this floor and into a comfy bed because we don't want anyone else seeing your stylishly grey underwear." They both laughed as I watched in awe of this nurse seamlessly manage to turn the scariest question into something so much more acceptable.

Naïve sent me to collect the intravenous medication I had stored away, appreciating I needed to feel useful, while she went out to her car to collect her bag. On her return she explained she was going to give Grace an injection to help with the pain and removed the pillows off the bed in order to make Grace as comfortable as possible. Within about fifteen minutes an ambulance arrived and Naïve met them at the door updating them on the situation. A mobile hoist was brought in and a loop placed around Grace's back to lift her allowing them to ease her out safely. The sheer skill and dignity they all used as they worked together, was admirable.

My parents arrived and my father brought the single bed downstairs into the front room, while my mother helped reorganise the furniture in the living room. Grace was hoisted into bed and made comfortable, while I made tea and found a plastic box to store the medicine and syringes. Within ten minutes the paramedics had packed up and left for another call, saying their goodbyes.

I carried a tray of tea into the front room, to find Naive and Fatima making Grace comfortable and settling her into the bed, dressed in her nightdress with her legs elevated on a pillow. Grace chatted to Fatima as if she had just called in for a coffee. They somehow managed to organise the whole unfortunate incident, into a manageable, less harrowing experience. Suddenly an auxiliary nurse called Fiona, came bursting through the door making her breathless apologies for being late. Her hair was windswept and her coat hanging half on and half off her shoulders as she tried, in vain, to prevent her bag from sliding down her shoulder. Fiona came out with a long story as to why she was late. She had arrived at the wrong house where an elderly lady had shown her into her elderly husband's room. She wanted help to wash and change his bed. Fiona said she put on her apron and gloves and helped the lady change her husband's pyjamas and put fresh sheets on the bed. "I didn't realise the mistake until I asked for the patients notes and the elderly lady said she didn't háve any. They had never had a home visit by the nurse before."

Naïve looked less than impressed. Everyone was quiet as Fiona continued her story rather apprehensively on seeing Naive's expression. Having concluded her story no one said a word, all attention was focused on Naïve waiting for her response. We looked like naughty children waiting to reprimanded by the teacher. "Anyway, I'm sorry, I'm here now, on the upside I think that lady could do with more regular help, those sheets were disgusting!" as she rounded off her apology."

After a few awkward moments we all burst into fits of laughter. Naïve looked at Grace, who was by this time, was hysterical and she responded diplomatically, that she would deal with the situation later but for now Fiona was to get on with the job in hand. Despite her professionalism, Naïve had a slight smile on her face. It was a timely reminder that despite what these girls did for a living, they were individuals with personalities and a life outside work. I don't think it ever dawned on me they would have to cope with devastating traumas like this in their own family lives and still be capable of carrying their job. They made us laugh in our darkest moments.

"No wonder people call them angels," I heard my father say to my mother, as she pottered around washing up. My father searched for tools to fix the bathroom door removed from its hinges in order to allow the paramedics to get access to Grace. I became emotional trying not to blink, I thought if I cried, I would never stop. Grace wasn't crying, she laughed away chatting to Naïve who had commented even with the swelling, Grace's thighs were still smaller than hers. She said had been on a strict diet for four months managing only to lose three pounds. In this atmosphere of normality, amidst the chaos, they managed to conjure up laughter and fun which was nothing short of breathtaking.

Naïve took me into the kitchen explaining Grace may have something called spinal cord compression, in layman's terms the cancer was pressing down on her lower spine. This had caused her to lose the sensation in her legs. Mum stood by me and squeezed my hand while she spoke, as if to remind me she was there for me, however feeling as distraught as I was. Naïve explained she had spoken to the doctor about possibly taking her into hospital however moving her wouldn't improve the outcome. She explained Grace's wish, was to remain here and because they were fully aware of Grace's prognosis, they were able to support her needs at home.

Things progressed rapidly over the next couple of days. We had visits throughout the day from various medical professionals and it was agreed if Grace suddenly went into a cardiac arrest, she wouldn't be resuscitated. It was a decision I was not and could not be involved in, but Naïve explained this was necessary so as to allow the team to continue nursing Grace in her own home and treat any symptoms. A formal agreement was placed in a yellow envelope and I was told to put it somewhere where it could be located in an emergency. I placed the envelope above the fireplace, next to the clock. I found myself hating that envelope; it was the letter to hell. At times I felt like ripping it up in the hope it would stop everything it represented.

I didn't leave the house for the next few days, friends and family visited with food and emotional support. The nurses came four times a day, supporting Grace with getting washed and changed into fresh nightclothes. They wrapped her legs in pads and bandages, as the swelling got worse. She had a catheter fitted and as the days past Grace slept for longer periods of time. The simplest of tasks became such an effort, she hardly had any appetite and they administered morphine on a regular basis to help cope with her intense back pain.

I slept on the sofa every night to be with her. She was petrified of the dark and needed the light or the television left on at all times. She kept a photograph of Charlie on her bedside table and I would regularly find it in her bed, where she had been staring at him, kissing his photograph until she fell asleep. I noticed she talked about him more than usual these days, in a happy way, asking me if I was proud of our beautiful little boy. She repeatedly told me how surprised she was that we had managed to make something so beautiful and perfect.

One particular evening she appeared more lively than she had been in days. She was wide-awake and chatting and asked me to open the blinds so she could see the moon through the window. She commented on the fact it was a full moon, a sign of change and new beginnings.

She mentioned she could see Charlie with a woman holding him in her arms, at the foot of her bed. She described the woman as friendly looking, with kind eyes, but wasn't sure who she was. The woman would say to Grace she was just taking care of him until Grace was ready to hold him once again. I put my head in my hands, she knew I didn't believe in the afterlife nonsense. She took my hands away from my face saying she knew I didn't believe her but it was true and she wasn't scared. I begged her to stop talking like that, it was too much for me to cope with."

'Maybe she just needed to talk about it," I interrupted. "Perhaps she did but I just couldn't," he answered. "You know Jacob, sometimes women are better at talking about their feelings than men. I don't think men are encouraged from an early age to talk about their emotions. Nigel used to ask me to talk to him in bed when he couldn't sleep. For a longtime I genuinely believed it was because he was interested in what I had to say but now I know it was because he was so bored by what I had to say it would send him to sleep. Bastard! Sorry... carry on, I didn't mean to interrupt your train of thought," I said apologetically. "No, Charlotte, I think you are right, women are better at talking about stuff that involves emotion, nurses are amazing at it.

I remember all this because one of the nurses, Emma, arrived at the house to care for Grace. She was chatting and laughing as she went about her work. She was telling Grace that earlier in the day she had seen a patient who had asked if she was Fatima or fat Emma. Emma didn't know quite what to say but explained she was Emma and she was actually on a diet. Grace, I remember, laughed out loud, she had the most charmingly, infectious laugh and while listening to her laugh, I realised I had not heard her laugh for such a very long time. Laughing was something we had stopped doing because our lives had become so serious. What a skill these nurses had Grace seemed so comfortable because she was able to laugh literally in the face of adversity.

I stayed in the kitchen as she washed Grace and changed her nightclothes. When Emma came in to fill a bowl of water. I don't know why, but I told her what Grace had said about seeing Charlie and a woman at the end of her bed. I thought she would confirm it was all a nonsense but she did the complete opposite. She said over the years she had nursed many people in their final days and it was common for the patient to say a loved one was in the room waiting for them. She went on to tell me about an experience when she was a student on one of the wards. She was part of the team doing the ward rounds with a consultant and a number of junior doctors. The consultant had gone into a room to examine an elderly lady who was in the last few days of life. He asked how she felt and if she was afraid. She answered saying, "I'm not scared, I know it's time, my husband and daughter are standing over there ready to take me with them." The consultant looked across the room to where these people were supposedly standing, and woman said, "There's no point in you looking, you won't see them they are not here for you, they're here for me." The consultant took her hand, smiled and left the room. The junior doctors followed him around like baby ducklings following their mother. The consultant asked the junior doctors what their understanding was of the patients who say they could see manifestations of loved ones in their final hours. A young Chinese doctor held up his pen to answer as the others uncomfortably searched through their notebooks. "It's chemicals, including endorphins released from the brain at the time of or close to death that make patients hallucinate. "Very good," the consultant said as they moved along the ward to the next patient.

Emma said she was disappointed by the answer; she wanted the lady to see her family and to know in death there was hope and something good on the otherside. She hated the scientific, clinical answer and had to tell herself to dismiss it from her mind as she continued to follow them on their rounds. As the junior doctors looked through the notes for the next patient, the consultant turned to Emma and asked her. "So now, tell me nurse why do patients see their dead loved ones and not cars, money or a big house?" Before Emma could answer he said, "It's because some things are bigger than us and thankfully it is impossible for us to know everything." Then he winked as he went back to join the ward round.

I was surprised by her story and found myself asking if indeed there was an afterlife, at least the possibility of some light in all of this darkness. Grace was such a positive person who saw only the good in everyone and everything. She believed in angels and karma. I loved the depth of her unfettered belief. I'm the total opposite; I'm so negative about everything. Grace would often comment I worried about things before they actually happened, always expecting the worst."

"Jacob, I remember once, my mother told me a story her grandmother told her about her life as a young woman. Her second son died tragically of pneumonia; he was only four years old at the time and had been poorly for a few weeks. She had tucked him up on the sofa with a pillow and a blanket while she encouraged him to drink plenty of fluid. She had gone into the kitchen so she could keep an eye on him through the net curtain covering the window. While she was washing up, she saw a pale figure of an old lady holding her son's hand, walking across the backyard and out of the gate. She dropped the pans into the sink, yelling as she ran into the living room, only to find him with his eyes closed on the sofa. He had passed away peacefully in those few moments."

"Charlotte I would like to believe in all that stuff but to be honest, I was adamant it was all nonsense, now I'm not so sure. Don't get me wrong I would love to be reassured Grace is living another life but honestly how can we possibly know for certain. Perhaps we will never know, otherwise we would each live our lives as if life itself was not precious. As we all do with everything, we think will be around forever, particularly if we know we have a second chance."

"After Emma had gone, that night we both sat looking at the moon until Grace fell asleep. I moved my chair closer to her bed, holding her hand as I continued staring at the moon for both of us. I wondered how anything she believed could be in the slightest bit true because there was no way she deserved what was happening to her, she had no bad karma to come back on her. That night I found closing the blinds difficult as I pulled on the cord to close them, I had the distinct feeling this would be the last time we would watch the moon together.

In the following days Grace slept most of the day and night, Naïve said because of her exhaustion she was going to set up a syringe driver so that Grace wouldn't need any further oral medication, she was too weak to swallow and so it was unsafe. Setting this up seemed to be a precise process, nurses were checking and double-checking the dosage for the machine to administer the drugs Grace needed to control her pain. Each nurse explained all I needed to do was to ring them if the alarm went off for any reason, a simple process, they made everything look so easy and straightforward.

Each night I would lie awake watching the little red light of the machine flashing every ten seconds, counting it as if it was warning everyone Grace's life was slipping silently away. The sound of the clock ticking on the wall was no longer background noise but a resounding thud, again reminding me our time together was ticking away. I decide to remove it from the wall and confiscated the batteries in an attempt to stop time moving forwards or at least the reminder.

I must have fallen asleep as I was suddenly awoken by the sound of someone talking; it was still the early hours of the morning and dark outside. It was Grace, she was talking in her sleep, telling me to place the pushchair in the back of the car and ensure Charlie was strapped in. She was smiling as she spoke aloud living out her dream. She said to make sure Charlie had his cuddly rabbit, she was sure he wouldn't settle without it. She giggled and smiled while she slept, as if she were part of a wonderful vision of what might have been. I tried to wake her by gently touching her arm but she didn't wake up. I shook her arm a little harder but it didn't work, she continued talking but didn't wake. I suddenly felt out of my depth and in a state of panic I rang the district nurse's number. They were apparently on a call in another part of town but would get here as soon as possible. I blurted out in desperation what had been happening and in one sentence she completely blindsided my fears. "Jacob, is it a bad thing if she is having nice dreams about her son? There is nothing to gain by waking her up to her reality. Try and take some comfort from the fact in her sedated mind she is having happy thoughts."

I suddenly released it was no longer a fearful world Grace would have to endure and the sad reality was now all mine. I felt so alone, more alone than I have ever felt. I was in such a scary place and nothing made sense to me anymore. Everything that had once provided me with any form of structure in life appeared to have crumbled below me, like faulty scaffolding. I realised I didn't even know what day of the week it was or even the date. Life's plan had disappeared and the once seemingly important matters, no longer meant anything at all. The house no longer felt like our home, furniture we had chosen together and worked so hard to pay for, now seemed totally irrelevant. Trinkets we had bought on our travels now became insignificant. Belongings had no value, I realised without Grace in my life nothing meant anything anymore. The post neatly piled up in the hallway by my mother, was wrapped in invisible ties and labeled with invisible tags that read, "open at a later date when your life is no longer in shreds and post becomes important again."

I went upstairs to wash my face and change my clothes. Clothes no longer hanging in order, just simply thrown inside the wardrobe and lying wherever they landed. I pulled out a creased t-shirt without a care in the world as to my appearance. I sat on the edge of the bed running my hands through my hair wondering where the hell I would find the motivation to even breathe. I noticed a large packet of painkillers on the side calling to me, a glimmer of hope the packet would end this pain. I picked it up and thumbed through the blister packs, I felt as though I was in some kind of trance, nothing in the real world existed. I went to the bathroom to fill a glass of water, and as I crossed the hall, I heard a giggle. I threw the tablets onto the bed and ran downstairs. Grace was still sleeping, smiling and giggling as she lay dreaming of a life, which was never to be ours to have.

# Chapter 11

Grace never fully woke up again and the next twenty-four hours were the longest of my life. She seemed to slip deeper and deeper into a sleep, no longer dreaming or laughing. Her body became like a breathing corpse, as if her soul was slowly leaving her body. I could no longer see the personality in her face; I knew the end was near. Her breathing pattern changed as she held her breath for longer and longer periods. At one point I found myself holding my breath with her and subsequently feeling the relief when she started breathing again.    The nurses explained breathing changes would be part of the process and there would be longer gaps between breaths. Despite their explanation I was resentful of every stage, life became a ticking time bomb, a living hell.

My mother and father looked in every few hours throughout the day, only for my mother to break down and cry and my father having to take her home. Every time I went to the bathroom, I noticed the pile of clean clothes my mother had put out for me with the slim hope I would shower. Showering, for a mum is a sign you are taking care of yourself and as the pile remained in situ, she knew I was not coping. She prepared my food, which she later binned, left untouched. She made me drink after drink, reminding me I needed to keep my strength up but what was the sense in that, just to watch my beautiful Grace fade away. I didn't want strength, I wanted God to take me so I would be there waiting for her. The thought of heaven became almost a paradise, a place where I got to be a father and a husband, without any of this earthly torture and not eating seemed to be a really easy option. Life felt as if it was over, I justified my need to die and now I needed to know for certain if there is an afterlife. If it existed, I would be waiting for Grace so she was no longer scared and if there was nothing on the other side, it wouldn't matter anyway. I felt nothing could ever be right in my life again.

There was a never-ending stream of nursing care, with Grace no longer capable of moving for herself, she had to be moved in bed to prevent her from getting pressure sores. She seemed comfortable and settled as they left each evening. She didn't flinch or make any noise while they moved her, otherwise she always seemed so peaceful and settled. I tried to talk to her that night, apologising for everything, as she slept. I begged her to wake up and not leave me, asking her what I would do without her because without her, my life would be empty. Let's face it I couldn't cook and couldn't carry on my life without her. I kept getting annoyed trying to initiate some kind of response, reminding her this was the house we both chose to live, telling her she had no right to leave. I was so sure she could hear me, Naïve did promise me the hearing was the last thing to go. She didn't respond I was so sure she was peacefully sleeping, while the red light of her syringe driver flashed away our lives.

I fell asleep only to be woken by the sound of the Alexa saying, "Remind Jacob to have a happy birthday and that Grace loves him so very much." It was the automatic voice reminder; Grace must have left it. I gazed down at my beautiful Grace lying so still, looking serene and peaceful. I touched her arm, she felt so cold. I shouted out, as the pain of reality thrust through me like a blunt knife straight into my heart. It was unbearable I thought my heart was going to burst. Agonising, physical pain ravaged through my whole body as if she was being ripped away from me. I sat on the bed and held her in my arms, it was all I had left. Her physical being was the only thing that prevented me from falling into the massive black hole which I knew was waiting for me."

As we sat on that roof tears cascaded down my face, I could see his pain engulfed him. I couldn't think of a single thing to say, nothing I could say would help in anyway. He was immersed in anger and grief, the love remaining with him had no where to go and had just turned into excruciating pain. Jacob found some kind of inner strength to continue his story, "I don't remember much after that except we must have been lying there for hours when the nurses called in at ten that morning. Naïve took care of everything with her usual professionalism. She walked in on my devastation without any shock or panic. She took off her coat and walked around the bed and gave quiet, simple instructions to Fatima. It was as if they went into autopilot. She gently took my arm from around Grace and told me it was time to let her do her work, giving me instructions to put the kettle on. "I can't leave her," I cried. "Please Naïve I can't let her go, not yet I'm not ready."

With a full sense of utter calm, she took my hand and said, "I know you're not, how can we ever be ready? It's time now Jacob, we need to make Grace comfortable. Now you go and put on the kettle and let me look after Grace. When you have done with the kettle, I want you to go upstairs and get me a clean dress and a clean sheet for her bed." She sent me off, like a boy running an errand for his mother. Within minutes she had contacted my parents. While I was in the kitchen, I could hear the nurses as I waited for the boiling kettle. They were talking to Grace as if she were still alive, apologising as they rolled her over to change her clothes. Naïve handled everything, it was as if she could read my mind as she combed Grace's thin, wispy hair and dressed her in a fifties style dress. She ensured Charlie's photograph was placed in her hands with her arms folded across her chest.

By the time I got back into the room everything was ready. Grace looked peaceful and beautiful. The bed and been lowered and my chair placed next to her. They packed up their things and went into the kitchen leaving me to have a few moments alone with Grace. I noticed the small front window was open and the cold air was blowing into the room. Fatima came back in the room to pack syringes into a box, apologising, as she opened the door. I asked her why the window was open. She told me it was an old nursing tradition to open the window to make way for the soul to leave and make its way to its final destination. She said she wasn't sure if she believed in it but wouldn't dare to be the first one not to do it, she had seen it done so many times before.

The peace in the house was quickly broken as my mother and father arrived, followed swiftly by my sister and her partner. I went in the garden to smoke a cigarette, while my mother said her goodbyes. My sister wouldn't go into the room, saying she preferred to remember Grace as she was. I couldn't believe they were already talking about my Grace in the past tense; she was already in my past.

I distinctly remember that evening my mother begging me to allow her to stay at my house but my father took her home insisting she leave me to be alone with my thoughts. I couldn't stand the idea of being around anyone; I just wanted to be alone with my grief. If people were around me I would have to pretend to be okay and I knew I wasn't, I just wanted to curl up and die. My mother had done everything she could but the truth was, nothing could take any of my pain away. I looked at her, remembering how it felt to let Charlie go. I would have done anything to keep him here with me. At that moment of course, I was my mother's little boy, she was feeling every bit of my pain, so it was for the best my father took her home.

The single bed was removed from the front room and the furniture put back where it once stood. The front room echoed with an emptiness the feeling of home had gone with Grace. I sat down in the armchair in front of the window hoping to see the moon as I drank my glass of whisky, but the sky was full of clouds and the moon nowhere to be seen. I went into the kitchen to re-fill my glass and the yellow sharps bin stood on the kitchen work surface looking prominent. There had been other sharps bins Grace had returned to the doctors following the fertility treatment. The last time Grace had returned one I remember the receptionist repeatedly questioning her as to who had issued the bin and why she needed it. She was asked to explain this while at the front of a long queue of people equally as interested in her private life. She returned home quite upset, feeling like she had just announced to the world she had failed once again to get pregnant, the bright yellow tub reminding her of her failure. I stared directly at it as I refilled my glass, then I picked up the bin and threw it across the room in pure temper and continued to stamp all over it. My temper increased, the more it appeared to be indestructible bouncing around the room, as if it was taunting me the more I stamped on it.

The weeks after her death were exceptionally strange. I couldn't make sense of anything. It didn't seem, real Grace was gone, I kept expecting her to walk through the door and start talking about the people she had met at work at any minute. I drank large amount of alcohol every night, often falling asleep on the sofa. One night I thought I heard Grace come into the house, she was singing as she walked in the front door. I sat up waiting for the door to open and for her to walk in but the singing stopped. I shouted out to her but she was no longer there and then I woke up realising it wasn't real. Sometime later, I remember I drove my car to the petrol station, noticing the fuel gauge was almost on empty, I started to fill up the car. I looked up to monitor the gauge and in the reflection I saw Grace walking across the forecourt and into the shop. I dropped the fuel nozzle and ran into the shop, checking all the aisles trying to find her but she was gone. The cashier came over to ask if I was okay, I asked him if he had seen her but he looked at me blankly and asked if I wanted him to ring anyone.

Grace had been gone four days, it felt like four years, I was living like a tramp. My house was a pigsty. My mother would come around and clean without a word of thanks from me. More often than not she would leave crying. I didn't wash or shave and I didn't eat, despite her best efforts to cook for me. I didn't want to survive I wanted to die. The drink took me to a place where I didn't have to think, with the hangovers allowing me to wallow in self-pity. I spent my days at the funeral parlour with Grace and the evenings waiting for the next day so I could see her again.

My mother called round late one morning quickly followed by my father and sister. I laughed; she had come with reinforcements. My Dad pointed out people loved and cared for me but I couldn't see past my own self-pity to care in return. "You have a funeral to arrange," my father said sternly as he picked up the whisky bottles from the floor and around the chair where I had slept all night.

My father's anger was evident. "This has got to stop son. The funeral director is calling at eleven and we are here to help arrange the funeral with you. I am warning you though, as much as we are here for you, I don't want your mother going home crying again today. She has been through so much, we all have, it's not just about you. Now go shower and pull yourself together and when your mother makes you a coffee, you thank her and drink it and thank her again." I didn't dare answer back or argue; my defiance only went as far as not answering him, so I went upstairs to shower.

By the time I came downstairs the room felt fresh and everything was tidy. My dad and sister sat in the front room talking and mum was in the kitchen sorting laundry. She handed me a cup of coffee and two painkillers for the headache she just knew I had. "Have you got any plans in mind for the funeral?" dad asked. "Funnily enough we planned for babies and holidays but never got around to finalising those plans," I answered sarcastically. My sister snapped at me reminding me dad was doing his best, as was everyone else. She said I was being childish and punishing everyone else was not fair.

"Well Jacob, I can understand them trying to help in anyway they can," I said in their defence.

"I completely agree" he said but I was angry and whatever they said at the time was going to upset me. I was somewhere I didn't want to be and was no where near ready to calmly accept my fate. No one in that room was coping, we put on a front and some do better fronts than others. Everyone has a tipping point, even my mum and dad.

"Jacob maybe it's a good thing we all have tipping points at different times, so at least we can help each other through difficult times." I said, feeling pretty pleased with myself that I had, for once come out with something sensible.

"The funeral director arrived and mum let him in just before she ran off to the kitchen crying again. He looked exactly as I had imagined, a small, bald man with a dark blue, somber suit. He shook my hand as he introduced himself. He carried a brief case which contained numerous depressing catalogues of coffins, flowers and headstones. As he spoke, I started to feel a little overwhelmed, inside I felt like I was screaming and wanted to run away. Never in my life did I want to choose a coffin for my wife. I didn't know when to say 'that is nice' or 'I want that one' because I didn't want any of it. We agreed and made out choice, none of it meant anything to me. It was sorted, everything organised and then everyone left and I was alone.

The night before the funeral I drove to the funeral parlour knowing this would be the last time ever I would be able to see Grace. As I pulled into the car park there was a funeral in progress. I parked up and walked around to the front entrance of the building, families were consoling each other in the entrance. I noticed there was a young woman; she looked hollow and haunted, with an ashen pale complexion as I walked around the back of the crowd and into the passageway. The receptionist requested I stand to one side as the bearers were about to carry the coffin through. The door opened and I stood back as a large man walked passed carrying a pink whicker baby's coffin. Men carrying flower arrangements in the shape of teddy bears and hearts followed on behind. That was it I couldn't take anymore.

Seeing Grace lying in the coffin had become somehow

normal. I pulled my chair closer to the coffin so I could sit and tell her what I had just seen. The room was dimly lit but comfortable. As I spoke to her, I noticed that a small gap in the curtain which allowed a shimmer of bright light into the room. As the sun came from behind the clouds it shone brightly onto Grace's face. The make-up they had applied to her face now sat on her skin as if it was an obviously separate layer. Her beautiful sleeping eyes looked more sunken and as I looked at her, devastation swept over me. It wasn't until that very moment I realised she was gone. I tried to shake her to wake her up, she felt stiff and cold, all her warmth had gone. I started to cry, begging her not to go, pleading with her to come back but I knew this was no longer my Grace; it was a shell of what she once was. I held her hand that day for hours and I kissed her, telling her I would always love her. I asked her to wait for me with Charlie and that I looked forward to being with her again. I had taken the quilt I bought for our wedding and covered her with it, telling her she was to keep it and show Charlie the pictures telling him about all the adventures we had. I placed her arm over the top of the blanket and her hand landed on the picture of us on a sailing holiday, an image of happier times.

Leaving Grace that day was intolerably difficult. Trying to decide when to leave was impossible. I waited until the sun went down before I kissed her for the very last time. As I got into the car my hand felt numb with the cold. I sat for a while trying to pull myself together before setting off home. The rain had been relentless all day but had started to subside, allowing the thick dark clouds to move and make way for the most beautiful pink sky I had ever seen. The last warming light of the sunset shone into the car and a warm beam of light shone directly onto my cold hand as I held the steering wheel. I planned to buy another bottle of whisky on my way home but found myself passing the shop, being too tired to go in. I went home, went straight to bed holding Grace's t-shirt while I fell asleep in a state of sheer exhaustion. Holding her t-shirt, I could smell her, it was the best part of my day. It was something of her that was still real. It gave me a slither of hope she was still here with me.

People described the funeral as 'lovely' and a 'beautiful service.' It was held at St Matthews; people came from miles around to pay their respects. My mother could hardly stand and had to be propped up by my father, while I carried the coffin supported by my good friend, Ollie. People crumbled as we passed them in the aisles. My mind took me back to the last time we were in a church and what a happy occasion it had been, our wedding. Carrying my Grace in a coffin was so surreal and far too much for my brain to process. We lay the casket on a stand at the front of the church and were guided to sit in the front row. No tears left my eyes, my whole body felt numb.

One of Grace's closest friends spoke at her funeral, her words muffled by her sobbing throughout. She talked of her kindness and her ability to make everyone feel comfortable. She spoke of her ability to always be there as a friend, as if she had an in built sixth sense when someone was in need. People in the congregation smiled as she spoke of Grace's gift at making cookies, her skills the envy of all her friends. She was joined at the alter by another friend, when emotions overcame her ability to speak. Together they reminisced about their beautiful individualistic, stylish friend who could make something special from nothing, often to the envy of everyone. Her quirky style was the order of the day, all of her friends wore fifties style clothing and headbands in respect of her memory. The funeral really passed in a bit of a blur but images of that day remain with me. I recall looking around at the faces of people and realising how many individual lives Grace had touched.

An elderly gentleman sat at the back of the church holding a single flower in his hand. He looked respectful and very smart in his shirt and tie clearly visible under his overcoat, with his thinning hair combed over to one side. I had no idea who he was but days later when I revisited the grave that single flower was placed on its own underneath all the large wreaths. I remembered Grace telling me about the old man who had cried as she served him at the stall because the flower on her gloves reminded him of his wife and wondered if it was the same man. I thought of taking the flower and drying it to keep but I couldn't, it belonged to Grace.

Suddenly Jacob was interrupted once again by the sound of a loud hailer bringing us both back to the reality on the roof. "We have trained professionals down here to speak to you. First and foremost, please raise your right hand if either of you are hurt in anyway?" It was a policewoman shouting through a loud hailer attempting to assess the situation. The sound of police radios could be heard crackling away in the background. I turned to Jacob, "They are asking if you want to talk to a professional?" He paused for a moment and wiped away the tears from his face. He replayed the sound of Grace singing on his phone "I just want to be with Grace, I want to be with both of them. I don't think I can stand the pain of being without them anymore,"

"They can help you Jacob," I said, trying to re-assure him. He knew that despite all the talking all the support all the turmoil in his mind, nothing would rescue him from the depth of his grief. "Where do you start when you have already had the best time of your life? I had the woman of my dreams in my arms and in my bed. She was everything, nothing else ever could come close. I don't want anything to come close because I never want to stop feeling this pain. Losing the pain means letting go of her and I can't do that," He said as he wrapped his arms around his stomach as if to hold back his physical pain. He sat quietly for a minute as the voice once again came over the loud hailer. "Raise your right hand if you are hurt in anyway?" I leaned around the air-vent and waved my left hand in an attempt to answer the question, indicating I was fine.

A voice quickly responded, "Does the gentleman intend to harm himself or others. Raise your right hand if he intends to harm himself and your left, if you are in harms way?" I got confused with the question and raised both hands then quickly put them down and raised the left. The crowd below began to increase with the sound of people screaming.

"Can you shuffle your way toward us Mrs?" the police officer shouted. I turned around and shook my head, I could physically but I lied, I didn't feel comfortable leaving him. I shuffled a little closer towards him, as the wind seemed to pick up. The cold air had still kept my legs feeling numb as I leaned forward and I held out my hand. "Please Jacob, take my hand let's get down off this roof?." I was shaking as I glanced down and saw the sheer drop below me. I felt dizzy and a wave sickness rose up from the pit of my stomach. Jacob was still sobbing, his full body shaking and his eyes were swollen and red with what seemed like years of built-up tears. I stretched out my hand and asked again.

"I can't move, Charlotte, I don't know how to jump or

how to stay. I don't have the strength to do either. I can't do it, I'm so sorry to everyone for everything." I screamed as Jacob stood up on his feet, balancing right on the edge of the ledge. The wind was howling around us both, my heart missed a beat in sheer terror as the tears flowed down his cheeks. He was visibly shaking throughout his body. I could hear the policewoman on the loud hailer behind me with the mixture of screams coming from the crowd below. "Please God, please don't jump, and don't end it this way, we can sort it, everything can be sorted. I know you can't do it yourself and I know I'm useless but I think we can get through this together. Please just take my hand, Jacob. Please I am begging you?" Finding the strength from the sheer panic of him falling to the ground below, I stood up on my feet and precariously walked the few steps towards him. I could see the empty vastness to the ground below. Jacob kept apologising over and over again for what he was about to do. "Please Jacob it's just me and you, we can give it a go. Please take my hand?" I held out my hand and my fingertips briefly met his freezing cold hand. "Come on we can do this together, please," I begged in utter desperation.

# Chapter 11

**Three years later**

I hate nothing more than public speaking and walking into this massive marquee only compounded my fear and hate when I encountered all the guests waiting for the event to begin. The marquee was huge, decorated with glitz, its chandeliers and tables adorned with huge, tall flowers and shiny glasses amongst the elegant table settings. Guests dressed in their finest clothes chatted frivolously amongst themselves, as the band played in the background setting the tone for the evening. A young man with a microphone headpiece headed straight towards me to remind me it was time for my speech. I was escorted up on to the stage where the young man pinned a small speaker onto my shirt. He reminded me everyone was nervous but once I was on that stage everything would be fine. I didn't believe a word he said and was horrified to realise I had forgotten my speech. I rifled through my bag to take out my bits of paper containing my keynotes, which were no longer in any order. Making sense of them suddenly became an impossible task. I could feel my mouth go dry with the nerves, my tongue practically sticking to the roof of my mouth.

I watched as people slowly started to take their seats at the tables, awaiting my presence on stage. A young man walked over towards me, thrusting a clipboard under my nose, reminding me I had a six-minute slot and not to run over my allocated time. He stated it would affect the whole schedule for the evening's events. Six minutes suddenly felt like six hours and the hope of a single word passing my dry lips would be a miracle. As I stood at the side of the stage I looked around for a familiar face and some kind of moral support. It was difficult to make out who was who because of the bright light on the stage and the dim candlelight of the tables in the front row.

The band started to play quietly, as if triggering a warning to the guests it was time to start. The muttering of the guests seemed to synchronize with the band. The lights of the main hall were dimmed and the lighting above the stage spelling the word **MINT,** lit up. The crowd applauded as the word glowed brightly against the dark backdrop. "You're on in two," the young man said glancing at me. I could feel myself physically shaking, as I tried to take a drink to lubricate my dry mouth. The room fell silent as I was ushered onto the stage for my big moment. The ruffling sound of me re-arranging my notes into some kind of order, seemed excessively loud close to the microphone. I took my hands away from the papers and awkwardly dropped them down by my side. The screen behind me flashed up the words **Minds in Need Together**, sponsored by Forsett Insurance. That was it, my cue to speak!

"Good evening everyone, my name is Charlotte and I would like to thank all of you for coming here tonight to celebrate the success of **MINT**. I would like to thank our sponsors, Forsett Insurance for organising this evening's event. The company have supported **MINT** and its development from infancy, helping us go progress an idea into the working reality it is today. Little did I know that the events that took place on the roof of a car park would trigger a chain of events that would change not only my life but the life of many others forever.

Almost three years ago, my day started out as any other but somehow, I found myself in the middle of someone else's crisis and suicide was their intention. At that moment in time, I felt utterly powerless and became entangled in the lonely, isolated world that is suicide. Although I felt alone and helpless, I was totally oblivious of the turmoil going on below, while perched on that roof and I had no idea of the number of people this whole incident involved. There was a policewoman with a loud hailer, part of a team of twenty police officers, numerous fire fighters and ambulance staff, working tirelessly to try and prevent a tragedy that day. Each with their own life experiences making them who they are, going about their daily jobs of rescuing people and saving lives. As we remained on that roof the emergency services were making plans for every eventuality, to ensure everyone affected was supported as much as was possible.

They did their utmost to protect others from being exposed to further devastation which at times, was absolutely unavoidable.

Families were informed and supported; plans were in place to access the emergency and supporting services as quickly as possible. People did what they naturally did, they did their best and I played my small part in all that.

If I may, I would like to tell you a little bit of how we, as an organisation, got started and the aims of our project. **Minds in Need Together** was developed and centered around the activity of sailing. The aim of the project is to provide space and support for people in need, while learning about how to sail and all that it encompasses. As you are most probably aware, suicide is the biggest known killer in men under the age of thirty-five and therefore our objectives are to provide a safe space to allow people time, offer support and ensure these individuals have the best opportunity to gain some form of safer perspective in their lives. We aim to support individuals throughout their lives by developing their own personal skills, listening to their concerns and where necessary, simply providing them with a safe place in their lives to be able to think more clearly. At the heart of our organisation is the prevention of suicide and I am sure we are all aware this has become much more prevalent in not only men, as I have mentioned, but generally among the younger population.

Our base is a simple boatyard, here on Dovebourne Valley Lakeside. Our humble boat yard that once resembled a shed is now, I am proud to say, a large and expanding business with a working staff of up to twenty-eight people at any given time. We maintain three boats on a full-time basis on the lake. They are each named the Dreamer, Grace and Pippa. We provide sailing classes and sessions for people of all ages and requirements. Our craftsmen provide education in carpentry, where individuals can develop new skills while socialising with others or alone, if they wish. We also provide sailing sessions for schools and recently, I'm extremely proud to say, for people with both physical and mental disabilities. Our coffee shop is open five days a week, which we are extremely grateful for but maybe not so much for our waist measurements, as Moira's cakes are totally irresistible. From our humble beginnings, we have had over six thousand visitors through are doors. I'm very proud to say the centre has become the hub for many other people in their lives. Even my cat Wilbur no longer stays with me at home, he has become the ships cat and spends his evenings in front of the log burner in the sailor's cottage utterly spoiled.

The pictures on the screen behind me and scattered around the room, will give you an insight as to where we have come from, where we are now and where we hope to be in the future, given your support. Please feel free to browse in your own time and of course there are members of our team available to answer any questions you may have. Thank you for taking time out in your busy schedules to visit our facilities. I would like to hand you over to Mr. Andrew Ross."

I walked from the stage feeling very proud of myself, despite my prompt notes being useless; I hadn't used them at all. I smiled with satisfaction, as the sound man patted my arm and said, "Well done, you didn't look nervous at all." I took my seat at the front of the stage to listen to old man Ross begin his speech. The crowd gave a rowdy round of applause as he took to the stage. Old man Ross walked up to the microphone where a photograph of a pretty young woman with the name Pippa, flashed on the screen above the stage, as he opened his speech.

"Welcome everyone! Before we start, I would be delighted if you would call me Ross, I have been called old man Ross at Forsett insurers long before I really was old and now that I am old, I am trying to get my younger years back! Ladies and gentlemen I would like to start by saying how proud I am to be here today in-front of this beautiful picture of my precious daughter, Pippa, the whole reason behind my involvement with **MINT**. It all started with an average day at work turning very quickly into a heart-breaking nightmare of a day for a number of people. A day that made a lot of people reflect on life. The feelings I had that day I hope I never have to encounter again but sadly such is life.

The beautiful woman pictured behind me is my one and only daughter Pippa, she died on her twenty-second birthday, a day she took her own life. She was a happy, young woman so her death was a great shock to everyone. We had no warning she was unhappy or any idea she intended to do such a terrible thing. She left no note but left my wife and I with our grief and so many unanswered questions. As a father or indeed any family member, you can never get over something as tragic as the death of your child, you just learn to live with the tragic circumstances and your loss. We have to move on, all too often carrying the grief along with us, like a chain around our neck. I had no incentive to do anything positive to celebrate her life until one momentous day, three years ago, I found myself on the roof of a car park. I had arrived at work that morning and was called to the top floor by a police officer, who explained there was a suicidal man perched on the roof. Immediately I switched to an automatic mode and organised a hub for the emergency services on the top floor providing whatever the force needed in the circumstances. I found myself hours later, unable to leave, I needed to know what was happening. I occupied myself helping make tea and refreshments for the emergency crew. I remember I was serving tea at one of the tables, when I saw a gentleman walk into the building and I knew straight away this was the suicidal man's father. His face said it all, I recognised the fear and hopelessness in his eyes. My heart went out to this man, I needed to do something that would actually make a difference.

Suicide is a part of a family's history but something not to be talked about. Suicide is very real and in people's lives right now, however suicide is something that can be prevented through awareness and the individual getting the right help at the right time. I promised myself I would do something and if I could help prevent just one person from feeling so desperately low, then it would help bring some karma to my own life. So, we went ahead and set up a suicide awareness program throughout my companies and then introduced the idea to other companies of friends and colleagues. I had the honour of being involved in the initial development of MINT, even learning to sail from the best, something I had never done or thought of sailing in my life. I learned to appreciate the tranquility of being on the lake along with the sense of achievement that comes with fixing things and working within a team. I am sure this haven will go from strength to strength, not only because of the support we receive from people like yourselves but also from the self investment of the people who come here on a daily basis, supporting others and providing some clarity in their own lives. On that note I would like to hand you to my good friend, David."

The screen behind changed to an image of a young man sailing alone on a lake. Not the cold, desperate, young man I had been sitting with on the roof that day but a smiling, happy man, enjoying a warm day sailing.

David began to speak. "I cannot thank everyone enough, for taking time out to attend this evening, may I welcome each and every one of you. The picture you see behind me, I am extremely proud to say, this is my son. That picture, without organisations such as MINT, could have been very different. My son is, thank God, alive and well and currently setting up another branch of the MINT boating service in Ireland as we speak, which is why he cannot be here tonight. Like Ross, I had no idea whatsoever that my son, who was recovering from the loss of his wife, would ever feel so low that death seemed like his only option. I was brought up in a world where suicide was seen as a sign of weakness or eccentricity, often hidden by families and perceived as some form of humiliation. Without all the amazing work of the emergency services and but for the beautiful Charlotte, today I would be telling a different story. When my son started this venture, I got involved as a father and a sailor, with no idea of how to relate to anyone finding themselves facing loneliness, depression and suicide. I am a man who gets his wife vouchers every year for Christmas and buys the same flowers from the same shop for her birthday. I have no imagination or insight as to how to support those with emotional issues. My idea of help would be to hide in the garden shed and smoke my pipe until all my problems passed. These days I find myself with people who want to talk about their problems or those who just want some peace and quiet and those who just need some space. Sometimes, asking such a simple question such as, would you like a cup of tea, or a cup of coffee or even would you like a mint, maybe enough to stop the clock and start the healing process. I have always considered the lake to be a most beautiful and peaceful sanctuary and to see people secure the benefits and enrichment of this idyllic setting, improves my life every day. I cannot tell you how proud I am of my son and how proud his wife, Grace would have been if she was here today. I hope this evening provides you with a small but memorable insight into the positive effects of my son's efforts. Someone once told me, there is good in everything and everyone, it is just a little hard to see it at times and some may need a little help to find it.

I hope you have a lovely evening; enjoy the meal and I believe there is some dancing later. One last thing, I think now is as good a time as any, to point out that everyone working here tonight, the chef, the staff in the kitchen, the waiters and the band are all involved in **MINT** in some way or another. They want to use this opportunity to put a little bit back into the pot of life and tonight it is their opportunity to show how thankful we are for your support. Your help provides us with the opportunities to change lives. I thank you."

The band started playing as David and old man Ross left the stage to a thunderous, standing ovation from the audience. Later I watched old man Ross with tears in my eyes, as he proudly danced with his wife, holding her close.

# Chapter 12

**Two years later**

I heard the shattering of glass breaking as I drove across the hard dirt track toward the boat yard. My car was packed full of supplies that I had attempted to squeeze in so that I only had to make one trip to deliver them all, instead of two. I wondered what exactly I had heard breaking, as I drove on trying to remember what I had packed and where in the car.

"Please…. not the jam jars?" I said aloud, as I envisaged the amount of cleaning up I would have to undertake. I drove around into the yard and parked in the overflow area in order to get a space. It was the most beautiful bright sunny morning and the sun glistened on the lake like shining crystals. There were already two boats out on the lake, as I arrived and an excited bunch of school children were sitting on the wooden benches in life jackets and helmets as one of the instructors tried to hold there attention to teach the safety-first instructions.

I could smell the aroma of freshly baked scones emanating from the café which immediately made me feel hungry and decide to postpone my diet until tomorrow. The full atmosphere of the place had a way of making me feel happy. People went about their business in the yard, chatting to each other as they passed. It was like coming home to a large family. I started to un-pack the boxes from the car, unloading the stock from the back seat first. "Thank goodness you're here, we are completely out of jam and I have got people sitting waiting for scones. Their tea is getting cold, I had to top them up with a fresh pot. I was going to send Jacob to the store but he is busy with two new starters," Moira said as she took over the un-loading. "I think some of the jars of the special black currant jam you ordered from the farm shop may have broken when I went over a bump coming down the lane," I explained.

"Surely not the jam from Withams? They always pack their products up so well, we've never had problems with supplies from there before," she replied, digging through the supplies to locate the jam.

We unloaded a few more boxes and piled them up close to the car.

"Found them," Moira said as she lifted the box from the car seat announcing only one was cracked and the rest were fine. "One casualty, we can cope with that," she said as she walked off carrying the cream and the un-broken jars of jam.

I stacked the rest of the boxes and placed them into piles to carry them across the final few yards to the boathouse. "Can I help you with those?" I heard a male voice ask behind me. "Yes please, if you don't mind, could you take that pile there to the main reception?" I replied, as I tried to balance three boxes in my arms glancing around to see who had offered help. I felt my cheeks burning bright red and my heart started racing. There, all of a sudden in front of me was a tall, gorgeous man with dark hair that matched his designer stubble. He had the most magnificent, blue eyes which made his smile more attractive. He lifted the heavy boxes as if they weighed nothing and headed towards the reception. I wanted to tidy up my hair with a sudden urge to smarten myself up but my hands were full. My hair band had become loose and half of my hair had fallen on my face making me look less than sophisticated. My outfit of choice that morning was an oversized sweater and leggings which didn't seem to be the best choice to offer a good first impression outfit.

I picked up three, much smaller boxes and headed towards the kitchen. "Who are the new members?" I tried to ask casually. Moira laughed raucously, "I knew you would like him. I knew it, the minute I set eyes on him this morning." "Well come on then, spill! What do you know about him?" I demanded. Moira put down her cloth and turned to face me, his name is Robert, he is single and used to be a soldier in Afghanistan, I believe. He is a volunteer, apparently Jacob met him at a conference earlier this year." Making a very poor attempt at telling lies, I told her that was all very interesting but I didn't find him in the least attractive and the true reason I had asked was a general inquiry about all new members. "Pull the other one it has bells on," Moira sniggered, as she carried on cleaning, laughing at my effort to hide my fascination and intrigue

I finished unloading the rest of the car helped by some of the school children seated by the jetty with a tea and scone. The day was gorgeous the sun shining down onto the valley and across the lake, the views were stunning, a perfect day for a trip out on the boat. I took my shoes off and allowed my toes to dip into the water. A small boat sailed passed and the crew waved and within a few minutes the wash from the boat splashed up onto my feet and up through the gaps in the wood of the jetty, causing my trousers to get wet.

"This is the most beautiful view, one can never grow tired of it," Jacob said appreciating the view as he walked along the jetty and sat down beside me. He snatched half of my scone which was coated in the greatest amount of jam and cream and proceeded to eat it in two mouthfuls, despite my attempts to stop him. He then continued to drink my tea. "Can't you get your own?" I protested "The scones aren't ready yet and I have to go out on the water in a minute. Do you want to see me starve? Anyway, your tea always tastes better for some reason," He said, as he laughed wiping away the cream from around his mouth. "Are you taking the new volunteers out?" I asked. "Yeah, they both have a little sailing experience which is good, but I just want to assess how good it is before they go out on the water solo."

Jacob looked at me, "Did I see a sparkle in your eyes Charlotte? Could that sparkle be for someone called Robert by any chance?" I protested, "Absolutely not, no not at all. I don't even know who Robert is and may I point out you are being utterly absurd as per usual, so childish, Jacob." Jacob threw a pebble across the water of the lake saying, "that's a yes then." He got up and left giggling to himself, and then pointed out I should do something with my trousers before I do see him, as I looked as though I had wet myself.

The rest of the morning I spent helping out in the busy coffee shop until lunchtime, when I stopped to eat some sandwiches back on the riverbank watching the boats go by. I could see Robert just across the lake, sailing with Jacob. The more I watched the more I liked what I saw. He had everything I liked in a man even though until that moment, I hadn't realised I had a preference for a certain type.

Over the next few weeks, I found myself finding excuses to visit the boatyard as often as I possibly could. This didn't go unnoticed by the staff who continued to make sarcastic comments such as, "you here again?" and "haven't you got a home to go to?" I found myself wanting to be around Robert and wanting to get to know more and more about him. In a few short weeks he had become a popular member of the team, and he sailed a great deal during his army service he had a great deal to offer the centre. His people management skills were found to be invaluable to the parties of teenagers who visited during the summer weeks, they seemed to gravitate towards him.

One particular lunchtime, I sat down by the river eating my sandwiches watching the boats go by and I could just see Robert across the lake sailing with Jacob. "Enjoying the view?" a voice from behind me said. It was Moira, she was carrying a package up to the car park for old man Ross. "Beautiful day isn't it," I replied, as I patted down on the grass in a gesture for her to sit down beside me. Half-heartedly she sat down, protesting she could only stay for a moment as she had so much to do. We sat watching the river enjoying the sun, quiet for a while, not needing to say anything in order to enjoy each other's company. We admired the view of the beautiful lake.

"Does Ross ever sail his boat?" I asked as I watched their sailboat bob up and down on the lake moored to the jetty.

"No, not too often," she answered. She paused for a while and said, "I don't think it was the sailing that was his main aim but more the challenge in returning her to her former glory. That is why the boat is named after his daughter."

"I have never really spoken to him about his daughter. What happened to her?" curious to understand the history. "I believe the boat was always about Pippa. He worked on it tirelessly, it was a labour of love. I remember how proud he was when she was finally launched."

"He declared; "I name this boat Pippa". May all who sail in her find the beauty of the lake reflected in their lives," as he smashed a bottle of beer onto the boat in his ceremonial naming tradition. He had worked on the boat since the yard was opened and had enjoyed every minute of refurbishing her back to her former glory. Named after his only daughter, he poured love and time into her restoration. She took pride of place, just off the jetty, where he would spend hours in his chair watching her in her rightful place on the lake.

Up until that moment in time he found it all too painful to mention his daughter and was notoriously private about her. Her death had understandably devastated both him and his wife, to the point they closed the episode of her life like a chapter in a book, too painful to resurrect. As the years have passed, it became even more difficult but in deaths own twisted way, facing the reality of what had happened to Pippa meant not remembering the good times either which left a huge void in their lives, which meant living was impossible and existing the only option.

Yes, all very sad, tragic, Pippa had been born to the Ross's late in life, they came to terms with the fact they could not have children. They even started embarking on the adoption process to offer a child a home and a place in their family. I remember them telling me at their first meeting with the social worker in their home, Mrs Ross suddenly became quite ill and had to go to bed and lie down. Mr Ross thought this was down to the pressure of the quite invasive procedures for the chance to ensure they were suitable for adopting a baby. The sickness continued for some time, so the doctor was contacted and after tests they discovered she was pregnant. They were over the moon; it was literally a miracle. Mrs Ross continued being very sickly throughout the pregnancy and was closely monitored by the doctors particularly as she was classed as an 'older mother'. She spent the final three months of her pregnancy on full best rest due to high blood pressure. She even left her job as a teacher. Their baby was so precious they agreed that they would take no chances with the pregnancy and would do whatever was necessary. Mr Ross being the only breadwinner worked extra hours as an insurance salesman, to make ends meet, eventually opening his own company. He would get up early every morning and prepare Mrs Ross a flask of tea and sandwiches so she wouldn't need to move from her bed until he arrived home. Every evening after work he would return home, prepare dinner and clean the house. His days were long and hard, often exhausted he would fall asleep in the chair at the end of the evening.

Pippa was born three weeks premature but a healthy weight of five and a half pounds, despite her term. They felt so blessed to have such a beautiful daughter. Mrs Ross remained a stay-at-home mum and within a few short years Old man Ross's company became successful enough for them to buy a larger house with a beautiful large garden. There was a small orchard at the rear of the house where they would collect apples and Mrs Ross would make homemade apple pies. Pippa had a happy, loving childhood with her parents immensely proud of her every achievement in life.

Growing up, Pippa was very quiet and contented but she struggled to make friends. She loved to read and sketch and would spend hours in a rocking chair on the porch of the house in the summer months, reading practically every book in the library. She was a slim child with mousey brown hair always kept in two braids. She had to wear glasses from about the age of four, to improve her sight and the other children at school mocked her for her thick rimmed glasses. She found staying on her own in school easier than trying to make any friends at all and so she remained the mocked child. She buried herself in a world of books, often coming home and telling her father the story she had just read. At the age of sixteen she decided she would train as a librarian. Three months before her seventeenth birthday she applied for a post to become an assistant librarian locally in town. She was thrilled at the opportunities of entering her chosen career doing something she loved so much. It was the day before her interview, she went into town to have her hair done ready for the interview, she thought she looked too old to go to an interview in braids and not a good look of an assistant librarian. Bravely she decided to cut her hair short for the first time in her life, choosing the look from a picture in a magazine at the hairdressers for reference. She kept her eyes tightly closed as her long her was cut short. She told the hairdresser she was so pleased she was going to rush back and show her mother. She left the shop and distracted by her refection in the mirror she stepped into the path of an oncoming vehicle. The driver tried desperately to break but Pippa was thrown across the road sustaining severe head injuries. People congregated outside into the high street to try and help her as she lay unconscious at the roadside. An ambulance was called and an unconscious Pippa was rushed to the local hospital. Her distraught parents kept a bedside vigil for over three weeks while Pippa lay in a coma.

Throughout the day and night Mrs Ross moved Pippa's joints, exercising her muscles, so as not to allow them to seize up. She would read to her and tell her stories of the adventures they had when she was younger. She combed her hair and washed her carefully around the tubes and wires which kept her alive. Their hopes for her recovery never faded and they were rewarded several months later when Pippa showed signs of some voluntary movement. First it was a simple movement of her fingers and after months of physiotherapy Pippa was able to sit up in bed and say a few simple words.

Fully aware recovery would be slow, the family made alterations to their home ready for her being discharged. They were just grateful Pippa eventually came home and was alive. They felt at home she would have more opportunity of getting better more quickly. They bought a wheelchair and had a path made through to the orchard so Pippa could have some access to her favourite part of the garden. An adapted swing was built on the porch, for her to enjoy the outside. Mrs Ross did most of the care and they employed a helper called April to assist. She was a young girl and despite her age she had a wealth of experience in this kind of situations. From a young age she had helped her mum and nursed her sister who suffered from cerebral palsy. Mrs Ross was keen for Pippa to have someone her own age she could relate to. After a few months at home Pippa's progress was almost remarkable. She no longer needed her wheelchair and physically could do most things for herself. Emotionally things were very different, Pippa developed a stammer when she spoke about something she found exceptionally frustrating. Her short-term memory was not particularly good following the accident and Pippa would lose her temper when she couldn't remember facts or appointments. Her once placid nature disappeared, she now appeared angry and frustrated. She founded it difficult to relax, finding solace only in reading. Her stammer became so bad that she refused to speak and carried a notebook to write down what she needed to say. She suffered from debilitating headaches since the accident but despite a great deal of medical intervention, and scans and what not, they couldn't see any further damage. Doctors used to say her recovery was already remarkable and things would take time. Mr Ross found the change in his daughter's personality really difficult to deal with and conversations would often end in arguments and days of moodiness and not speaking. Pippa would spend days at a time in her room, refusing to see anyone. The whole family attended counselling, although Pippa tried her hardest not to engage. After three months of weekly sessions the psychiatrist determined there was nothing they could do and this was how Pippa would remain and it would be best if the family try to deal with the reality of how she is now and not live in the hope of any further changes.

Things did improve a little with Pippa eventually taking a job as an examination monitor in the local school over the summer. She seemed happier in herself although still blighted by headaches. Her pain medication was increased but the downside was she was no longer allowed to drive because of the medication. Pippa found herself once again dependent upon her parents and a small part of her freedom and independence was taken away. She was advised to have regular eye tests in case the medication harmed her sight. Pippa's headaches improved but she continued to attend routine eye appointments. Then she was told her eyesight had deteriorated since the last visit and there was the possibility, she may lose her sight in the not-too-distant future. To everyone's surprise, Pippa seemed to take the news in her stride. There were no tantrums or mood changes she just said, "What will be, will be" and she never mentioned it again. The Ross's felt a little unnerved at her response. The following morning Pippa went off to work as usual, with three examinations to facilitate that day. Mrs Ross dropped her at the school and went to do her weekly shop followed by an appointment to go to the hairdressers. April was at the Ross's home cleaning and due to collect Pippa when she rang. During the afternoon April said she heard a car pull up on the drive but when she looked to see who it was, she only saw a car pulling away. Thinking it may be someone just turning around in the road, she thought nothing of it until later when she went out to hang the washing. She walked down the garden carrying the wet clothes in the basket however she had forgotten the pegs, she walked back to the house just as the phone rang. Expecting it to be Pippa for a lift, she answered only to find it someone trying to contact Mr Ross about work. She went back to attend so the washing and as she hung the clothes on the line, she saw something that would haunt her forever. Pippa hanging, lifelessly from a tree at the bottom of the orchard. Distraught April ran trying to desperately lift her from the noose around her neck, but she was too heavy. She frantically ran for help but no matter how quickly everyone arrived, Pippa was already dead, nothing could be done to save her. Her distraught parents handled the death with dignity, supported by the people in the village in which they lived and worked. They opened a small memorial garden for Pippa with swings and climbing frames for children from the village to play. People left flowers at the garden, helpless to support in any other way for a family suffering such an unimaginable loss. Suicide was not something that was discussed and often perceived as a blight on the family. The coroner, an old friend of the family, concluded her death was as a result of un-intentional suicide as Pippa's decision making would have been largely affected by the medication she was taking. Mrs Ross always thought this was not true and that her decision to commit suicide was probably something she had thought about many times before but not succeeded in the conscious effort to put thoughts into action. She once found a large stockpile of medication hidden under Pippa's mattress while cleaning her room and when confronting her about it, she broke down saying it was a silly whim of an idea at a low point in her life and had quickly seen sense. Pippa made her mum promise faithfully not to tell her father about the incident at the time, a decision Mrs

Ross would later regret come to regret. Old man Ross felt caring for someone with suicidal tendencies was like trying to put together a jigsaw puzzle where the pieces changed every time, thereby preventing you from ever getting a clear picture. Suicide was something they simply could not face." Moira then concluded "They were living a parent's nightmare at a time when suicide was seen as a disgrace."

I felt an overwhelming sadness for them knowing the details of how Pippa had died and for a few moments we sat in contemplation.

Moira eventually stood up saying, "come on this is supposed to be a happy occasion, we have birthdays to celebrate."

It was Sunday and we were planning a birthday barbecue for old man Ross on the riverbank. He rarely attended events to celebrate his birthday, he much preferred the company of the sailing team. His wife, Arianne, worked in the kitchen, initially volunteering for one day a week but quickly became a daily routine. Today was no exception, she was helping in the kitchen to marinate the meat and prepare drinks and salad for the evening's celebration meal. One of the volunteers had offered to play his guitar providing the entertainment for the evening alongside the band who accompanied him at weekends. Tables were set and heaters placed ad hoc around the seating area.

Everyone was doing their bit for the birthday celebrations.

Everyone contributed to his birthday present they had chosen a director's chair made with his name on the back which he could use to take his usual place on the jetty and admire the view in his own chair. The chair was placed on the Jetty with a large bow tied to the back with a birthday balloon attached that floated in the air. The jetty had recently been built on the riverside close to the boathouse and old man Ross, as he was affectionately known, had been overseeing the construction work. "Ohhh! he will love all of this," Arianne said as she stood behind me holding her cup. "I think this place has actually given him his life back and certainly given us our marriage back. He had become an empty shell of a man after we lost our daughter. He threw himself into his work and became a very successful empty shell of a man. However, money doesn't buy the things that count in life, does it? The building and coordinating the construction of the jetty and the managing of the yard has provided him with a kind of purpose to get up in the morning he now has a passion for life. He comes home and tells me about all the new people he meets and looks for various ways to help them. He is constantly networking trying to find employment for these people here at the yard, helping them to move on with their lives.

Unfortunately, we could never help our daughter, we

didn't really get the opportunity, but I think he sees the opportunity here and it has brought my old Ross back to me. I heard him in the kitchen the other day and he was singing along to the radio. That was the first time I had heard him sing since she died. People here have become our family we are so lucky. So here we are after years of building up million-pound businesses, we have found some happiness in building a wooden jetty on which to place his throne."

The party that evening was amazing. The weather was warm, the food was as good as it smelled once the barbeque was alight. Jacob and Robert claimed title as the chefs of the barbecue under the close supervision and direction of Moira. Drinks were poured from large glass, serving jugs filled with the most incredible fruit filled punch. The fire pit was constantly topped up with logs which glowed as the daylight faded into night. Old man Ross proudly sat in his chair taking charge of the fire pit as Arianne provided him with food and refreshments, having to remind him he wasn't really a director and she was certainly not his maid.

I poured a drink and walked barefoot along the old jetty, which looked rickety and small in comparison to its new replacement. The water on the lake was calm, it shimmered just like reflecting glass and the sound of rippling water played like music. The moon seemed larger than usual, as it hung in the sky over the stunning views of the lake and the valley beyond. Time seemed to stand still as I sat there. The warm air blew around my bare legs, while the water splashed over my toes as I wriggled my feet in the water.

"Isn't this the most serene place in the world?" Robert said, as he followed me along the jetty. "I've made you a coffee, thought you might like one. Do you mind if I join you?" He asked as he handed me a mug. "No not at all," I tried to answer calmly struggling to contain my excitement at the fact I was actually speaking to him. We both sat bare foot, with our feet in the water. The water only just covered my toes in comparison to his fully submerged feet because he was taller than me. "There is always a warm stretch of water here in comparison to the lake. I don't think we will get that on the new jetty. Are you going to dismantle this one?" I asked. "No, we talked about it but Jacob said it was not so much about mooring the boats but about a sanctuary for people. When you are here all day there is always a steady stream of people who just come here to sit. Ross wants this jetty actually re-enforcing and a rail added, so it becomes more accessible," he answered. "Do you like it here, at the boatyard, I mean?" I asked. "I have loved it. It's the sense of community that makes it for me. I lost all that when I left the army and I hadn't realised it was such a huge part of my life until it had gone, and there was a large void in my life."

"How long were you in the army?" I asked. "I served eleven years altogether, I hurt my leg skiing, otherwise I would probably still be there." "Why did you come here then? Why Mint sailing?" I asked. "I met Jacob at a support group for ex-servicemen and women when he was giving a talk on emotional wellbeing. He mentioned you and how he had attempted suicide one day on the roof of a car park. He seems such a genuine bloke, really inspirational."

"Did you try to kill yourself?" I asked, then quickly apologised realising the intrusive nature of my question.

"No need to apologise, fair question. No, I didn't but two of the men I served with for a number of years, did. Men, who I had always considered to be strong, never thinking it was something they would ever contemplate in a million years. They both had so much to live for, neither of them ever openly talked about depression. I saw the devastation they left behind and how their families struggled to pick up the pieces afterwards. One of the men was my best friend at school, the young lad standing over there with the dark hair, is his son. His name is Reece; I brought him here because he has struggled with coming to terms with his father's death. He has only been here a few weeks and I can already see a huge change in him. His mother was at a loss to how to help him. He had been missing school and isolating himself from everyone. She found suicide notes he had started writing and subsequently discarded. He was just a young lad and let's face it, as adults we don't know where to begin to make any sense of it, so I can totally understand why he has no idea how to start to move on. He was angry with his father, angry at the whole situation really. Anger can turn into behavioural issues if it is not dealt with, so here we are, starting with sailing. Strangely enough, he has enjoyed working with the men building the jetty, more than the sailing. He has been spending a great deal of his time in the workshop. I think he may have found his vocation in life. He even made his mother a wooden tray the other day and she was in floods of tears."

"Was the tray that bad?" I asked, and we both laughed. "To be honest it was a bit rough" Robert replied, laughing. We both sat quietly for a few moments but curiously enough it was a comfortable silence. "In a strange way, helping him is helping me, it takes my mind off thinking about me I don't think I had started to grieve until I came here. This is why places like this help people so much."

"Funnily enough, I was going to ask if you had come here with your wife, to the boatyard I mean?" I asked, my heart praying his answer was no! The fact he wasn't wearing a wedding ring, he must be single. Trying not to be too overt, staring at his muscular arms in his tightly fitted t-shirt, I wondered why on earth he would ever be single and then decided he must be a womaniser. My mother always said you should never trust the good-looking ones and he certainly did fit that category. Seconds away from full on drooling, I was snapped back into the conversation as he said, "No I'm not married, I'm single."

I could hardly control the smile that swept across my face at his response, until he followed up with, "I was engaged to be married a couple of years ago, but things went wrong and we split up. The wedding was arranged but it wasn't to be," he sighed, his words with a tone of regret. No longer smiling I said it was a shame, obviously not meaning one single word, however I imagined some modelesque, beautiful, blonde with legs to her neck and a three-inch waist. Robert looked deep in thought and sat in silence for a few moments. I quickly apologised for asking such intrusive questions, unveiling his feelings on such a sensitive issue but he insisted it was fine. "The memories haven't gone far enough to dig up, they are still there, every minute of every day." "Wow! You must have loved her a great deal?" I wondered. "Who?" he enquired, as if we were suddenly in two different conversations. "Your fiancé," I answered. "Oh, you mean Emily, yes I did at one time but now we are just good friends. Some things are never meant to be. She's married and lives happily in New Zealand with her husband. They are expecting their first child later this year, things are going well for her." I felt a sudden relief, she was no longer a part of his life. "How about you Charlotte? Have you ever wanted to tie the knot?" he said grinning. "Only every day of my life since I was about sixteen, I dream of my wedding dress on a daily basis. I've decided if I'm not married by the time I'm forty then I am going to rent a groom for a wedding day." I said, laughing. "I think there's a web site for that kind of thing," he answered and we both laughed.

We watched a group of children in their canoe's giggling away as their boats crashed into each other. Then Robert started to talk about how essential it was for Reece to have somewhere like the boat yard. He said that he hadn't realised just how much time and space he needed to start some kind of recovery. "There's just something about the river that is so beautiful and being around these people here makes it all that bit more special" he said, as he looked out over the water. "May I ask why Reece's father took his own life?" I asked, albeit sheepishly, quickly followed by re-assuring him he needn't need to answer my intrusive questions. He didn't seem too concerned by my question and began to tell me the background story.

Apparently, Reece's father, Jack, was nicknamed Union which came from his service in the army. Robert and Union had served together as young squaddies and were very much the best of friends. Union was supposed to be best man at Robert's wedding. Union was taller and broader than Robert, with dark hair. Robert said he was a charmer with the ladies and the uniform made him a 'babe magnet'. Union loved to flirt with the ladies but it was only ever a game, just friendly banter. He was in love with his childhood sweetheart, Katie for as long as he could remember. When they were stationed abroad he would read her letters over and over again and carry her photograph everywhere. He would proudly show off her beautiful picture at any given opportunity.

When he found out she was pregnant with Reece, he was ecstatic, life took on a whole new meaning. He started taking professional-driving courses in the army to get qualified and work towards a trade and leave the forces to be with his family. Union was always the life and soul of the regiment. Younger recruits looked up to him and the older soldiers respected him. He could lift the spirits of the lads with his jokes and his positive outlook on life in general. Union was the glue that held the squadron together.

It was the second week of one of our tours, some of the more senior soldiers volunteered for an outward-bound survival course, the course as the title suggests, required camping and marching across rivers and mountains. They both went on the course and it was in the evening of the fourth day of the course, having endured a 16-hour exercise, they returned to camp. "Oh! that camp sleeping bag looked like a welcoming five-star hotel bed!" They were all messing about laughing and joking most of the night and they cooked meals on the fire. Everyone was extremely tired and retired early in preparation for the early start the following day.

That night Union returned to the tent he shared with Robert and another soldier saying, "Well lads that's a wrap I thank you all for your excellent company. It has been a pleasure. I'm off to bed. I think I need a good, long, beauty sleep." The other lads joked about needing at least three weeks to improve his looks and Union went to his tent smiling at the comments he had just provoked. That night was like any other, it wasn't until the first light, life was to change forever. Robert apparently awoke to see Union's bunk empty and he reached across to feel it, it was cold and had obviously been empty for some time. Robert stuck his head out of the tent and could only see the dusty embers of the campfire, so he got dressed and walked across the hillside to the river on the far side for some fresh air. The river was flowing fast from the heavy rain. Robert stood by the river and went to drink water from his canteen, which was empty, so he bent down to refill his flask and a green flash caught his eye. He couldn't breathe as he tried to shout out words which wouldn't leave his mouth, while quickly wading into the ice-cold water. He was trying to reach Union who was walking deep into the river. Robert waded out losing his unlaced boot as it filled with water. The strong undercurrent of the water pulled him over into the wrong direction. He managed to scream out to Union begging him to stop but his cries were either not heard or ignored. By now other soldiers had woken up and were rushing to the riverbank. Robert waded out even further as a boulder, thrown by the strongest wave, landed on his foot breaking his bones. Between the cold and the shock, Robert felt nothing and carried on reaching out to his friend, who by now was standing in water up to his neck. Robert tried swimming towards him but was held back by the current. Screaming Union's name as the noise of the water attempted to silence him, he kept trying to swim against the tide to get to him.

With one turn of his head, Union was no longer visible. Pulled away on a wave like a rag doll, it was useless Robert even trying to reach him. Robert persistent in diving under the murky waters over and over again, coming to the surface to catch his breath and screaming Union's name. Other soldiers started forming a human chain to reach them but the current was pulling Robert further away. Pure adrenaline kept him diving into the murky water again and again, this time he hit his head on a rock as he went down. He felt himself being pulled onto his side and further under the water as the current took him down river. He reached out to try and find anything to hold onto when he felt Union's hand grab his. In a state of panic, he swam as hard as he could holding on tightly to his hand pulling them both upriver to relative safety. The current was so strong the weight of Union pulled them both further under the water, Robert struggled to hold his breath, his mouth full of muddy water. Robert said he saw his whole life pass before his very eyes just before everything went black. He gripped on tight to Union's hand and it appeared to be the end for both of them, when all of a sudden Robert was apparently hauled back with a random hand by his t shirt. Two soldiers yanked him out of the depths of the river while Robert continued to hold on tightly to Union's hand. They shouted for him to let go as they tried to pull him to safety but Robert knew he could not let go. After what seemed like hours, they were both dragged up into the shallow waters. Robert struggled to stand up in the freezing water as the other soldiers tried to force Union's, now frozen hand apart from Robert's. The freezing cold temperature had forced Union's hand to close shut around Robert's and breaking his fingers was the final act that eventually separated them. Robert watched in a state of shock as Union's mud-encrusted body was raised from the river by five of his regiment. His body lay at the side of the river wrapped in a blanket. Robert sat by his side also wrapped in a blanket, as the blood from his head wound trickled down his face to meet his tears. He heard the corporal mutter the word, 'suicide.'

"I never knew he ever felt like that, Charlotte. I didn't realise when he said goodbye earlier that night, he meant forever."

"All of those years we spent doing everything together and I never in a million years knew he felt that bad. I can picture him now getting inside the tent laughing like he didn't have a care in the world and all the time deep down he was suffering."

I couldn't think of a single word to say could dignify his statement.

"It will remain with me forever the fact that I let him down and that I was not there for him when he needed me the most." He paused for a moment, quite obviously very upset by the traumatic memory. "I can still see him every day, walking into that river but in my dreams, I'm walking alongside him, and I never seem to be able to save him. At his funeral, his coffin was swathed in the union jack flag, Reece still thinks it's his dad's flag made in his name, in his honour. I could never say to him son, there is no honour for him in suicide, it is a silent illness."

We remained on the jetty until the sun went down and the warm breeze was replaced by cold night air. We talked about everything and anything as the river splashed around our feet. I draped a scarf around my legs as the breeze became cooler, not wanting the elements to prevent us continuing our conversation. I felt comfortable around him. I felt comfortable with him. Even the long pauses in the conversation felt relaxing and not in the slightest bit awkward. The man I had half-heartedly fallen for, had turned from the untouchable soldier to a softer, more gentle man with a broken heart. A part of me had hoped if I got to know him, I would like him less because the fear of moving into a relationship was inevitably going to end up with me having my heart broken, which was a fear I felt unable to face. I attempted to change the subject into something a little lighter and asked if he had always wanted to be a soldier? He looked like a soldier and talked like a soldier so his answer threw me. "No, not at all, as a young man being a soldier never crossed my mind. Don't laugh but my dream for years as a young boy was to be a bus driver. I loved buses I was obsessed with them. My uncle once took me to London to see the buses and I swear I was in bus heaven," he said recalling a trip that made him smile. "I love London," I said enthusiastically. "I went with my father for my eleventh birthday, he had friends in the city, so we stayed at their home for the night. My father knew London well, he used to work as a black cab driver when he was younger, so he took me to meet some of his friends who still work the cabs. It was fascinating, they all had their stories to tell. Oh, and I remember my dad's claim to fame was he once played guitar with one of the Beatles." Robert laughed shaking his head in disbelief. No, it's true, honestly. The black cab drivers have these small wooden huts which they use for their breaks between fares and a few of them go there and jam on their guitars. They said they often had famous people pop in for coffee but the most famous of all was one of the Beatles who would down regularly. He even had a signed parking ticket that said, 'bad luck but good music' signed by PMc." "Well, I'm seriously impressed that is some claim to fame," Robert said smiling.

"Did you know the black cab drivers do all kinds of fundraising activities for charity, they never charge to transport families to Great Ormond Street Hospital wherever the fare is from. There is some kind of a pact between them all that they won't charge for families using the hospital at Great Ormond Street, that seriously impressed me, still does to be honest." "You are a wealth of information, Charlotte, fascinating."

"Come on then tell me why you became a soldier and not a bus driver, because the two careers are miles apart?" "It's not an exciting story, nowhere near as exciting as jamming with the Beatles. Well, when I was six, my mother left home, I came back from school one day to find my dad sitting on the armchair with a bottle of whisky ripping up a note she left. She packed up everything and went while he was at work and I was at school. She took my younger sister with her and evidently didn't look back, My father wasn't interested in me I got in his way most of the time, eventually he sent me to live with my aunt and uncle and their three kids. I became the youngest of four boys in a cramped three bedroomed house." "Why did your mum leave you behind?" I asked.

"Truthfully? to this day I have no idea; dad never

discussed it and destroyed the note she left behind. My aunt said she never had "any kind of life" living with my dad but would never really stay anything else. I always hoped she would come back for me but she never did, so that was that." Robert seemed very matter of fact about his childhood as if he had come to terms with being abandoned by his mother at such a young and critical age. "Did you never hear from your sister?" I asked. "No not at all I imagine she must have a family of her own. I really hope life has worked out well for her." "It is all so very sad, Robert, you must have so many unanswered questions." "No not really. I think I found my own family in the army with the lads, particularly with Union. I joined the army when I came across a poster in the job centre, it was entitled 'Band of Brothers' of all the random things, that stayed in my mind. My aunt and uncle were good to me but I didn't really belong with them I was always an outsider and then after my dad died, I decided to go straight down to the local army office, literally an hour or so after the funeral and signed up. The rest, as they say, is history and I became a soldier." "What about your girlfriend, Emily? Why did that end if you don't mind me asking? He went quiet for a while; this was obviously an area that was still a sensitive issue.

He went quiet for a while; this was obviously an area that was still raw to him.

"Emily was a nice girl she was everything I thought I

wanted, at a time when I really had no idea what I wanted and went along with everyone else's expectations of me. When Union died, I struggled for a long time with the direction of my life. I drank far too much and was not the easiest person to live with. I fell out of love with life and out of love with her. She couldn't understand why after Union's death I couldn't move on, so we eventually called it a day and she left. It was for the best, looking back, but I think it was inevitable, Union's death just made it happen sooner than expected." "Do you think you will ever see your mum and sister again?" I asked. "Do you think you will ever see your mum and sister again?" I asked.

"I'm not sure, maybe, one day I might. I used to be really angry with my mother particularly as a teenager but not now. Life throws you so many curve balls you can never really judge anyone else's decisions regardless of the ultimate consequences. I believe we do what we can in order to get through life and my mother did what she felt she needed to do. I had a small hope that when I passed out from the army she would suddenly appear and be proud of what I had achieved but it was stupid, she wasn't in the crowd of crying mothers on that day. Mothers are supposed to be around at the most important times in your life, aren't they?" "Oh god! that's awful," I found myself feeling upset for him. "Before you start pitying me, my Uncle was at my passing out parade, standing proudly in his Sunday best, so I wasn't alone." "How about your aunt? Did she not go?" "No, she died of cancer just before I signed up but, had she been alive, wild horses wouldn't have kept her away, any excuse to wear a hat," he said chucking to himself.

Robert told me more about his time in the forces and about the comradery he experienced. We laughed when I told him about my chaotic relationships and the blind dates I had 'suffered' and the embarrassment of it all. That evening we were last to leave the boat yard and he walked me to my car, despite the fact it was only twenty yards away on the lower drive, and he politely said goodnight.

I drove home, my jaw aching from the mere fact I couldn't stop smiling. I felt like a character from an old English novel as I glided around my bedroom smiling and singing to myself. I showered, percolated a coffee and made a cake, ready to relax on my sofa ending the poignant evening in a state of mental bliss. "Are you in?" I heard a familiar voice shouting. My peace was shattered as Linda Shepell from Flat 14 across the hall, let herself into my flat.

"Obviously, Linda as you can see by the door left on the latch. To what do I owe the pleasure?" I asked sarcastically. "Oh, you are in your dressing gown, I do apologise for the intrusion but I wondered if you had a number for the on-call electrician, the lights are flickering as though my flat is possessed, it can cause epileptic fits you know. I'm not prone to illness because I come from a very robust gene pool. My grandmother lived until she was a hundred and two you know and that was practically un-heard of in her day."

"Yes, Yes, Linda, you have mentioned it before at least once or twice," I said rudely interrupting her. She was famous for her ability to ensnare you into a conversation monopolised by anecdotes from her very tedious life. Linda famously, had her heart broken on three separate occasions in her life and since then she had become a modern-day Miss Havisham, breathing only to warn others of the dangers of heart.

I took the electrician's number down from the notice board in the kitchen and handed it to her, warning there may be a hefty call out charge and that it might be best to turn off the lights, go to sleep and call them in the morning. However, she didn't listen to a word I said, she continued babbling on about nothing of any interest. I walked to the door holding the handle shepherding her towards the door. She completely ignored me, pushing past me and made a beeline for my bookshelf, squealing in delight at the fact I had the very book she had been hunting for, right there on my shelf and that she would love to borrow it. She grabbed the bright, yellow covered book from the shelf totally overwhelmed by her discovery. "This book could change your life, the author is the guru on relationships, people flock to her for advice. Oh! you have made my week, I'm simply going to have to read it by torchlight right away, I can't possibly wait until the morning. We need to plan a girly night with a nice bottle of red, we obviously have the same taste in books as we do in men."

I couldn't think of anything worse than spending a night discussing either books or men and with her of all people. I escorted her out of the front door, insisting she keep the book; it was my pleasure. She continued to rave about the book and its author even as I closed the door behind her desperate to see the back of her. I heard her giggle with excitement as she shouted, "night!" from across the hallway.

Linda's intrusion had ruined the peaceful atmosphere for the evening. As I lined up the books she had left lying on the shelf, the titles brought back the memories of the disastrous relationships in my life. Titles such as, 'How to keep your man happy' and 'Learning to be a better woman.' reminded me of all the self-doubt and disappointment. The earlier feelings of joy and happiness turned into questioning how foolish and ridiculous I was, I was acting like a silly young teenager. One relatively short conversation with an attractive man and I was allowing myself to be drawn in again. I felt myself becoming angry at letting my shield down and revealing signs of weakness, it was therefore no surprise that women like Linda would see a connection between us, perhaps I was a younger version of her. I tried to remind myself of the fact I had moved on with my life, I had a better job in the firm, I am respected by my colleagues, even by the 'Dylan's' of the firm albeit reluctantly. I was happy with what I had achieved, I had been able to avoid most of the deception and allurement of being in a relationship. Eliminating every notion of Robert from my mind, I decided living in the real world and not the world of a love-struck teenager, was my way forward. She reminded me I was the worst at relationships and the last thing I needed now in my life was a man, no matter how handsome he was.

My intentions were all good but Robert was the only thing on my mind, in the best possible way. What had started as boat yard related texts, turned more personal in nature. My phone never left my hand, communication from Robert was my priority. One evening he had text and asked if I had any plans. I tried to wait before rushing to reply in an attempt not to sound too keen. After checking my watch at least ten times, I replied saying no plans and he was welcome to call over for a drink. I quickly jumped in the shower and then rushed out to check to see if he had replied. My excitement went to the next level and I giggled like a silly schoolgirl, smiling at the screen as I read his reply.

'On my way!' he texted. I practically screamed with excitement as I rushed to change into something sexier than my flowery pyjamas and my mother's old dressing gown things were looking up! I spent the following morning trying to convince myself I was a modern woman, completely happy, in control of my life, and content with a one-night stand, so I ignored Robert's texts that arrived throughout the next day.

Over the following weeks I spent less time at the boat yard and more time at work. My absence at the yard did not go unnoticed; I received numerous texts from Moira and Jacob asking whether or not I had fallen off the planet? I made excuse after excuse, blaming my workload, much to my disappointment because I honestly missed being at the yard. Planning the expansion of the boatyard kept me busy at work, there were issues regarding the entrance to the yard which required special permission and planning consent as the area was in an area of protected natural beauty. There was an old quarry on the hill above the boatyard site. It had been abandoned for years and trees were now growing restricting access to the site. It had become a popular route for walkers where the river had been eroding its way through the quarry, carving a stream out of the rocks. Heavy rain had increased the stream into a more vibrant outpouring of water and a pool had established itself at the base of the stream. It was a popular area for families to picnic, while their children swam in the pool, heated by the rays of the sun. We had as a committee, visited the location with old man Ross and the officers from the local planning department, to establish how we could use the space to increase the footprint to the entrance of the boatyard, without intruding onto this developing area of beauty. There were growing concerns raised over the fragility of the slate on the ground.

I needed to undertake a site visit at the boat yard however I was confident Robert was firmly banished to the back of my mind and I was, once more a woman in control of my life with no need of a man. The morning I arrived there were numerous lorries parked alongside the top of the bank just below the quarry, preventing me from parking in the allocated boatyard car park. I parked at the top just behind one of the lorries hoping that my car wouldn't be in anyone's way and walked down the bank and across to the boat yard. Moira was the first to point out how I had not been down in a while, as I entered the café, captivated by the smell of her famous scones. "Oh! so you're still alive then?" she said sarcastically. "Yes! Obviously! I've been busy with work that's all," I responded, almost trying to convince myself it was the whole truth. Moira walked across and placed a huge, sumptuous, warm scone and a piping hot mug of tea in front of me at the table, and said "Charlotte, there is no point in running away from life just because you are too scared to face it, it will either catch up with you anyway or worse, pass you by. Either way you have to face it." "I can assure you Moira I'm not running away from anything, I have been busy, that is all," I replied sternly, further cementing my lies.

I could never deceive Moira, I'm sure she could read my mind. Moira was the kind of woman people migrated towards; her very presence represented a welcoming charm. She knew everyone's business and was the master of confidence. You could talk to her about anything. She was a 'cosy, homely type,' from the aroma of the cakes she baked, to the hot tea she constantly had brewing for everyone when they needed it. She would light the log burner the moment she arrived in the morning at the coffee shop, to ensure everyone following her in came experienced a warm welcome. Her tearoom was her pride and joy. If it wasn't for the fact, she relied on a lift home every day, I would honestly swear she lived in that tearoom. The tearoom was very much the centre and focal point of the hub. She had seen that many tears and smiles from her customers in that tearoom, she could write a book about each and every one of them and it would be a best seller. She wasn't the most attractive of women, she looked older than her years, with her short, dark, curly hair and dark circles underneath her eyes, as if she hadn't slept well the night before. Her clothes were plain and served only as a backdrop to her flowered apron, which she wore like a uniform with pride. I knew precious little about her background and assumed she had never married purely because she never wore a wedding ring. I interviewed her when she applied for the job initially in actual fact, she was the only applicant. She impressed us all with a plate of scones she made and as a result was offered the job immediately while we tucked in to a second helping of her scones and copious amounts of her home-made jam.

She made the tearoom her own and it successfully grew into a thriving enterprise at the boatyard. She would announce the menu of the day first thing in the morning scribing it on the chalk board, which often made my mouth water at the idea of her delicious food. Old man Ross even built her a chicken coup at the side of the boat shed where she kept rescue chicken from the battery farms. Her chickens were her pets, she nursed them back from the brink of egg producing exhaustion, she adored them. They all had their own individual names and she insisted they all had their own personalities. She started out with only two but she caught the bug and two soon became 22 and a new coup and run was needed as she would often take in more and more. Every time we ate an egg sandwich, she would point out they were her hen's fresh eggs, from her girls, as she called them. She would box up eggs for everyone to take home, reminding us they were from happy hens identifiable by the bright yellow yolks of the eggs.

"Seriously Charlotte why are you avoiding that lovely man, Robert, you know you could do much worse you know?" she said. "Oh, thanks Moira, you make me sound like third prize at a best in show and for your information I am not avoiding him, as I told you before, I've been busy!" I said, I thought rather convincingly. "Pull the other one, it has bells on! You are avoiding him and you know it." She could read me like a book. "Moira, I just don't want to fall into a relationship, I am so bad at them. I have 'break my heart' written right across my forehead, I swear."

Moira just looked at me, like a mother waiting for a child to finish her tantrum. "And he has issues!" I said as if needing to justify my comments by way of a defence. Calmly she replied, "Don't we all dear but that doesn't stop life from passing us by if we're not careful. He likes you I can see it in his eyes. He has been miserable since you started staying away from the boatyard." Wise words as always from the lovely Moira. "Have you ever married, Moira?" I asked curiously.

Moira started wiping the already immaculately clean surfaces as a way of detracting from my intrusive question. "Marriage was just not an option for me, dear. Now don't get me wrong, there is nothing wrong with marriage, it's just not for everyone. Anyway, when I was younger my time was taken up caring for both my parents. My mother, in particular, wasn't a well woman and as I was an only child there was only me to help. My father was a proud man, I nursed him for over three years until he unfortunately died, the last few months of his life he became a shell of his former self. My mother could never cope with him really and eventually herself became bedridden after his death. I had to give up college to look after her when it all became too much. My mother was ill for a lot of years." "Did she die from cancer?" I asked. "No, I think she gave up after he died, she simply could not live without him."

"What were you going to do a college?" "I was going to be a nurse ironically I succeeded before I even started a course, I nursed both of my parents, which was a privilege. I like to think I did them proud, they were both well cared for."

"Moira you gave up your life for them that is a big deal," I said feeling the greatest respect for her.

"No I didn't, I chose to take care of them, just as they had cared for me and that was my choice in life and I'm pleased I had the opportunity to do that. So many people die lonely and uncared for, it breaks my heart, it really does."

She sat down at the table, wiping her hand on her apron smiling as she spoke, "I was in love once his name was Harry, we went to the same school he lived in the house three doors down from us with his family." Moira smiled as she described this 'cheeky chap' she had fallen in love, with fair hair and blue eyes. He once brought her flowers freshly picked from his garden and wrapped them in old newspaper. Her eyes lit up as she described the long-stemmed pink roses she

227

proudly placed in a vase and stood in the front window for everyone to see. When her mother became ill, Moira would occasionally sneak out and meet him at the allotments and he would often leave her fresh vegetables he had grown on the back step. Even preparing the vegetables, she said would make her smile, knowing he had thought about her that day. I asked her why the relationship didn't develop any further and she answered, "it was just simply not to be." Despite her hardships Moira had contentment in life which I secretly envied. Unlike me, she didn't seem to stumble along through life trying hard not to accept things which became inevitable. She talked about her work in the boat yard and how she loved cooking at night preparing for the following day she said it provided her with a purpose. She mentioned the friends she had made while working here and that she enjoyed hearing about the interesting stories and the tales of the intriguing and fascinating lives of those she met over the years. "None of us are really alone, all our lives are entwined, whether we like it or not. That's why the boat yard successfully supports so many people, each of us make up just a little part of what we all need to fulfil our happiness. Shutting yourself away in the hope it will shield from all the disappointments you amy never have won't work, Charlotte, life will just pass you by.

You see everyone who comes here in some way have something in common the understanding life is precious and can change at any moment. Life is for living and not hiding from." "Well the words 'pot and kettle' come to mind if we are talking about shying away from emotions," I said as if I just had an epiphany.

Moira looked shocked replying, "I'm sure I have no idea what you are talking about. I have scones to bake, hurry up with your tea, I want to get cleared away ready for lunch."

Moira would always get flustered when scones may be burning in the oven as they were usually timed to perfection.

"You know who I' m talking about. I've seen you and that Ron who works in welding? Don't tell me you haven't seen him, he' s working on The Sea Mist engine in shed three?" I said laughing. At that very moment Jacob walked into the café and grabbed half of my scone. "Your old man is in, Moira, I think he is a keeper, he's finished that welding for me," Jacob said laughing.

Moira flushed with embarrassment saying, "Shsh! the pair of you, you're being daft, I simply forgot about the scones that's all, it's been a busy morning and I have no idea what you two are talking about and don't wish to know."

Jacob laughed, "She sure does know, she has been over to the shed four times already and I even heard a rumour Ron was offered tea in the best china cups and if I'm not mistaken, none of us are allowed to go near."

Moira shuffled quickly into the kitchen telling us we were acting like a pair of kids and she had run out of clean cups nothing more. At that moment Ron walked into the tea room leaving Moira in such a tizzy she dropped her tea towel on the floor. "I've welded the door back on the entrance to the hen run for you, Moira. You should get a few years out of it and it won't swing open in the wind again.'

"Why thank you Ron much appreciated. I've made you a meat pie for dinner and mash potatoes with beef gravy and put you a tub together to take home," her eyes sparkled as she spoke told him.

Ron was not a looker; he dressed like a man at least ten years older much like Moira. He was a widower and had thinning grey hair. I watched them, envious of the obvious chemistry between them. They quite obviously, enjoyed each other's company. It made me believe perhaps some people are destined to be with each other.

Moira was smiling from ear to ear as she walked back behind her counter to fetch my favourite jam. "Well then Charlotte, I suppose you aren't interested that

Robert has been asking about you each and every day you have been away and he's also here today, doing repairs caused by the floods. We could have done with your help actually; the rains have been dreadful, we had to cancel over twenty training sessions in the last two weeks. The repair shop has been swimming under three inches of water at the far end of the workshop where they do the welding. It was all hands-on deck quite literally, moving equipment to a safe height away from the flooding, even the cat has taken up residency in the hub near the log burner!" I felt a tidal wave of guilt flow through me and tried to justify my absence saying I had spoken to Jacob and he had said nothing about the problems with the rain. "No well he wouldn't, would he? he was trying to give you some space. Personally, I think you need to stop trying to read into every move in life and just learn to live it. This precious little act you're putting on, doesn't wash with me." Moira stormed off into the kitchen stating she had 'said her piece' and "just leave it at that."

I didn't feel like eating my scone following the dressing down I received, so I wrapped it up in a serviette and left the café. I felt my heart jump as I caught sight of Robert across the yard, he was stacking the canoes onto the trailer. He waved at me as I, perhaps somewhat over keenly, waved back with the scone in my hand. "Hello, you," a voice behind me said, as Jacob came up and kissed me on the cheek. "Nice to see you back." "Don't you start! I have just had it all from Moira. I've been busy at work that is all. If you must know I think we may have cracked the plans for the expansion work with the quarry owners," I retorted. "Well, I hope they hurry up because it's murder trying to move cars and lorries around here. I've had to cordon off an area at the top of the bank in case any of the children due to arrive on the next minibus wander over there. This rain has made it treacherous up there. Oh! and one more thing, Robert has been asking after you, he's worried he scared you away."

I burst into a false sense of laughter, it was so false, I could hear my inner self, trying to claw it back with embarrassment but failed badly. Jacob stared at me, as if I was having some kind of outer body experience. He grasped my hand, cupping my fingers, as if to re-enforce his sincerity. My raucous laugh thankfully now winding down in the deafening silence into which it escaped. "Listen to me for once in your life, we both know you like Robert and he likes you. If that's even as far as it goes then it is something but you have to stop running away from the first sign of a relationship, like you are jumping out of a boat that is about to go over the waterfall." I started to get upset on hearing his honesty but couldn't reply, I couldn't argue with what he had said as it was true. "You are beautiful, you deserve to be happy. You are not cursed you're just scared. Robert is a great guy; you should give him a chance. We both know, probably more than most, that if you don't grab life by the horns and live it, then it will grab you by the ankles and drag you down. Life happens regardless of whether we live it or not. I'm the living proof we are not all doomed to failure, look how well things have gone for me." "Oh! Jacob, I wish I had your confidence, I'm just so scared I'll mess up my life again,"

Cars and trucks had started to back up on the driveway to the boat yard which caught Jacob's attention as he, once again, kissed me on the cheek and ran off to sort out the parking. I saw Robert run from the far side of the yard to help Jacob. I started smiling once again just at the very sight of him, unable to control my feelings any longer.

"Charlotte, can you move your car, it's in the way." I heard Jacob shout from the top of the bank. By now Robert was moving one of the lorries a few feet so that he could move another to try and unblock the access which was by now completely blocked. Two lorries were heavily laden with support beams heading towards the quarry, they had become stuck. One Lorry was to be unloaded with the help of the forklift truck before either of them would be able to move. The space in which they would usually have turned around had become blocked with fallen stones following the heavy rain and the path was much too narrow to safely reverse.

I got into the car and started the engine, reversing

slowly. Jacob waved his hands in the air as if signaling for me to stop. He then walked off forty yards or so towards a truck further up the road. I sat patiently for a few moments enjoying watching Robert running from truck to truck in an attempt to clear the road. I lost sight of him a few times as I tried to twist round from using the wing mirror to the rear-view mirror to see him working. I was distracted when I leaned across towards the passenger side of the car to get a better look.

I glanced up a second or two later when I saw Jacob waving his hands frantically in the air as was running towards my car. I heard him screaming and shouting, then a thunderous, bang shook the car. Suddenly I felt a huge thud, as my car was shunted at the front, pushing my car round a further six foot across the pathway. Simultaneously the thud was followed by another gigantic bang when tons of slate fell across the bonnet of my car, shattering my windscreen. It all happened so fast I didn't even have time to scream. I felt a sharp pain in my neck and legs as they were crushed with an added deluge of slate. I could hear people screaming around me, everything suddenly became one big blur, dust clouds bellowing everywhere, I could hear huge slabs of stone collapsing and cascading down the hillside. I tried to open the car door and drag myself out but the weight of the slate weighted across my legs was too heavy and the pain in my neck was excruciating.

After what seemed like forever, the dust started to clea and people appeared to be gathering around the car. My ears were ringing but I could hear the faint echo of voices mumbling, and the sound of people trying to remove all the rocks and slate. The dust cleared slightly revealing a huge, dented, blue lorry, the back of which was smashed beyond all recognition, covered in slate. The lorry must have taken the brunt of the collapsing wall. An overwhelming fear hit me like a tidal wave as I remembered seeing Robert jumping into the lorry, moments before the disaster.

It was interrupted by pain shooting up my legs, I held my breath until the worst of the pain had subsided and waited nervously for the next one. My instinct told me not to move, however I couldn't move even if I wanted to with the weight of the slate and rubble on top of the car I realised even if I could move my lips and shout out, it would be futile. I could still hear voices coming from different direction all around me but I couldn't understand or place them. I tried to work out which direction my car was facing and where Robert would be but I couldn't get my bearings. I had cuts on my hands bleeding profusely and two of my nails had been ripped from my fingers. I couldn't understand how my hands didn't feel painful. I could the sounds of a siren in the distance and the beeping as a truck was reversing. The car suddenly shunted and dropped from the back, I thought I had screamed out however no sound left my lips. I completely froze and held my breath, while the

.t seemed, in an attempt to find its balance, as if
very edge of a cliff, about to take a plunge at any
d, I felt a grappling pain across my stomach and
to gently loosen my seatbelt. It felt as though I
in some kind of parallel universe, looking down
:ing myself in situ. Petrified at the thought I was
ead and this was my afterlife experience. Then another
pain shot across my stomach again hauling me back to
reality. I yelled out to Robert, this time the words left
my mouth. I heard voices answering but I couldn't
make out what they were saying as were muffled. I so
desperately needed to speak to Robert, I wanted to
know he was alright. The idea he may seriously hurt
was terrifying.

I felt a hand on the back of my neck, as a paramedic
stretched through the broken windscreen. "She's alive
and talking," He shouted, quickly followed by the
sound of relieved voices behind him. A blanket was
arranged to the side of my head when I heard a loud
crack resound near my ear, as they used their machine
to remove the roof of my car.

"I'm here, Charlotte, I'm right here with you," I heard a
tearful voice shout. "Robert?" I managed to mumble.

"No, it's Jacob. Don't worry about Robert, they're
looking after him. Listen to me Charlotte, it's important
you keep really still. We're going to get you out of here
as soon as we can I'm right here and I'm not going

anywhere," his voice was comforting. "Is Robert alright I need to know he is ok?' I asked desperately. Jacob paused before he replied, "They are doing everything they can and he has the best team in the world helping him." Even in my disoriented mind, I knew his response meant it didn't look good. Arms seemed to be reaching over at me from all sides of the car a collar was wrapped around my neck and a blood pressure machine on my arm. Padding was slipped onto my hands to prevent any further bleeding and all the while Jacob remained at my side speaking to me. The noise of the machine cutting into the roof had stopped I heard murmurs of some kind of problem.

"I'm sorry Robert," I said out loud.

"It's Jacob, remember and you have nothing to be sorry for, just keep calm and try and relax," he insisted. "Please tell him I'm so so sorry, I do love him it just scared me," I said trying hard to get my words heard clearly. "He knows Charlotte, everyone knows. You two are the worst kept secret ever. When this is all over you can tell him yourself," he promised.

"I told him I didn't want to see him anymore," by this time I was sobbing. "Trust me, Charlotte, he knows how you feel, everyone in this yard knows you two were made for each other we having all been waiting for you to come to your senses, that's all."

A paramedic leant into the open space, which was at one point the car window, to explain they were going to move me shortly but he needed to give me an injection before they could do anything. "You won't feel a thing, I'm going to put the injection into your thigh, don't be afraid," he said as he was given the syringe. "No! I'm….." my words faded. Inside my head I tried to speak but the words were incapable of moving anywhere.

"I'm pr……." I tried again in vain.

I heard Jacob's voice frantically pleading with me to speak. I tried but I could no longer tell if my lips were moving or whether the words came out. I felt so sleepy.

"She's pregnant," Jacob shouted in desperation, as I drifted away, unable to stay awake.

Then there was nothing, apparently, I was air lifted to hospital with internal bleeding I had fractured my left leg, had severe conclusion and trauma wounds to my arms and face. However, I had such a lucky escape; nothing short of a miracle. When I woke up, Jacob and my mother were sitting at my bedside in the hospital. My mother abruptly burst into tears then warned me not to speak and to just try and relax and rest. I looked over at Jacob and my question was written all over my face, "what about Robert?" "Robert saved your life, Charlotte," Jacob whispered, as he held my hand. "Is he alive?" I sobbed. Jacob's eyes were bloodshot, obviously red from his tears, "It was touch and go for a while but hopefully he is going to be okay. He has a long way to go but it's already looking better than any of us ever dared hope. He reacted so quickly when he saw what was happening, he saw a wall of slate starting to collapse and slide down towards the car, so he reversed his truck just in the nick of time, crashing your car out of harm's way. The fact he reversed so quickly probably saved his own life as well yours because the back of the lorry took the brunt of the avalanche." "Did I cause this chaotic disaster by leaving my car parked, blocking the top road?" "No not at all, it was all a consequence of the torrential rainfall. Robert literally rescued the whole situation from developing into something so much worse." "He literally saved your life," I could hear my mother weeping, as I found myself drifting back into a deep sleep.

# Chapter 13

One year, eight months, two weeks and three days later.

The warm breeze sailed along the dusty stone passageway of St Matthews Church. There was a beautiful smell of freshly cut grass drifting through the air. The sun shone through the stain glass windows of the church and I could hear chattering in the pews of the church. Children could be heard rushing around and playing with excitement. As I stood in a small, stone side room of the church, I took a deep breath as I gazed at my reflection in the mirror, there was a loud creek as the aged wooden door opened quickly and in walked Jacob. He looked incredibly handsome in his navy suit and light blue tie. I wiped a tear from my eye, trying so hard not to disturb my make up. "Why the hell are you crying? This is supposed to be the happiest day of your life," Jacob said as he took a tissue from a box on the table and wiped my eyes. "I don't even know why I'm crying. I miss my dad but what if I'm not doing the right thing? How do people even know if they are doing the right thing, I mean getting married is a big deal, isn't it? It's forever, isn't it?" I blurted out hysterically. "Well, it's not forever, there is always divorce but that is a party for another day. A wise woman once told me, people never really leave us, they are always with us somewhere, so I'm sure your dad is here with you." Jacob said smiling. "Please Jacob, take this seriously I'm a mess and an emotional wreck. What if this is all too soon? People say once you get married everything changes. People who have been together for years split up as soon as they get married, it's a well-known fact. Or what if I don't go through with it and I blow my chance at being happy? Oh God, what do I do?" I sounded like a foolish idiotic woman. "A wise woman once told me nothing happens by chance, everyone is provided with opportunities and we each choose whether or not to take them up. Robert is a great man and you two are perfect for each other. You are so happy when you are with him, why on earth would you even begin to have doubts now?" He asked.

"Now all my make-up is wiped away and I look like a panda, my mascara is everywhere," I remarked, as I took the tissue from his hand and wiped my eyes.

"You look more beautiful than any bride I have ever seen," he said, as he glanced over my shoulder into a large mirror.

I was touching up my makeup and adjusting my dress as a woman's voice from outside the door shouted to ask if everything was ready, as it was time. Jacob answered for me saying we were as ready as we would ever be. The distant sound of birds singing outside, were suddenly drowned out by the organ music being played in the chapel. This is it Charlotte, it's time you look beautiful. Panic came over me like an all-engulfing wave. My legs turned to jelly and I could feel my face turning red. I told myself repeatedly breathe Charlotte, breathe as I panted like a woman in giving birth. "Please Jacob take my hand, I can't do this without you." I said in desperation and sheer panic. Jacob took my hand and with the other reached into his pocket and took out a small box wrapped with a bow. He placed it in my hand and closed my fingers around it. He lifted the back of my hand and kissed it. "Thank you for letting me give you away. Thank you for everything." I loosened the ribbon and opened the small box, inside was a gold bracelet with a charm in the shape of a sweet in a wrapper. "It's beautiful," I said feeling myself start to cry again. Jacob clasped the bracelet around my wrist.

"You offered me a mint that day on the roof at a time in my life when I was in a very dark place and I couldn't see any sign of hope in the world, you brought me back to understanding the realities of life. You were there when I needed you and regardless of my total lack of faith in God and fate, I believe you were truly heaven sent. You didn't just save my life; you saved the lives of all those I could have hurt forever. You know what? I don't think even after all this time, I have actually said thank you, Charlotte. Thank you for giving me back my life and helping me to see the wood for the trees." Jacob's eyes filled with tears as he took a hold of my hand, "Take my hand Charlotte, let's do this together," he said as we turned to walk towards the main door of the chapel. Conveniently overlooking the mascara, I held on tightly to Jacob's hand as we stepped out into the chapel where the wedding march echoed from every corner, Jacob squeezed my hand as he calmly walked me down the aisle, watched by the awaiting congregation.

The mixture of the organ music and the whispers amongst the guests, commenting "doesn't she look stunning.?" lifted my confidence. I glanced over at Jacob as we walked slowly down the aisle towards the alter, his eyes were focused straight ahead, he had pride written all over his face. I could feel my own tears of joy so I tried to breathe deeply and started blinking rapidly to prevent any more of a mascara disaster. I saw my mother as I arrived at the front pew, wearing the enormous pink hat, she had taken so long to choose, she certainly stood out from the rest of the crowd. To my right, I could see my husband to be, Robert, looking as handsome as ever with Reece, looking very grown up, standing at his side. Reece's mother struggled to contain her tears watching her young son, standing with honour as a growing young man. Reece was best man standing where his own father would have justifiably stood. He wore his father's medals on his army cadet uniform to honour his memory. I walked slowly towards Robert as he smiled, waiting to marry me.

Robert's smile looked almost radiant as we turned to face the priest. The chapel went quiet as the organ stopped playing and the guests stopped talking. There was a harmonious lull in the air as the priest asked, "Who gives this woman to be married?" "I do" Jacob said, as he offered my hand to Robert. Jacob then turned around to take his seat at the pew next to his fiancée and their baby girl, Lottie Grace, who held her arms in the air to greet her daddy enthusiastically.

After the vows had been exchanged and sealed with a kiss we both turned to the ovation from the congregation. We walked back down the aisle, taking our first steps to start our new journey in life as Mr and Mrs. Robert kissed my hand just like a prince with his princess, joy and happiness flowed through me, like blood through my veins. Nothing was ever going to ruin my amazing life, both as a mother and a wife my dreams had become a reality.

As we reached the foyer of the church covered in confetti and rice, I notice a blonde female, standing waiting just outside the entrance. She wore a pale blue suit with a colour co-ordinated, wide brimmed hat tilted over to one side. I thought she must have been one of the wedding guests however she wasn't wearing a corsage, unlike all the other guests, she looked as though she had been watching the ceremony from the entrance. Robert immediately stopped, as if in a state of complete shock, gripping my hand tightly and said, "mother?"